SABOTAGE THREATENS MIKE MARS —AND THE SUCCESS OF PROJECT QUICKSILVER

Here is the second novel in the new MIKE MARS space-adventure series.

Mike is chosen to fly America's latest rocket ship —the X-15——but before he can make the test flight, the danger of sabotage rears its deadly head.

As the count-down nears, Mike desperately searches for the phantom-like figure of a man with a cruelly scarred cheek. He knew he had to find him, or Project Quicksilver would be lost!

AND DON'T MISS *MIKE MARS AT CAPE KENNEDY*—COMING NEXT MONTH!

M.A.R.S.

MIKE MARS FLIES THE X-15

by DONALD A. WOLLHEIM

Illustrated by Albert Orbaan

PAPERBACK LIBRARY, Inc.
New York

PAPERBACK LIBRARY EDITION

First Printing: June, 1966

Library of Congress Catalog Card Number 60-14181

This Paperback Library Edition is published by arrangement with Doubleday & Company, Inc.

Paperback Library books are published by Paperback Library, Inc. Its trademark, consisting of the words "Paperback Library" and associated distinctive design, is registered in the United States Patent Office. Paperback Library, Inc., 260 Park Avenue South, New York, N.Y. 10010.

Special Acknowledgment Notice

THE author extends his personal thanks for the valuable assistance rendered him in the course of preparing this book by the United States Air Force, the National Aeronautics and Space Administration, and North American Aviation, Inc. Particular thanks are due to Major James F. Sunderman, of the USAF Book Program, to Captain James C. Sparks, Jr., of the New York USAF Information Office; to the many persons at the Air Force Flight Test Center who extended me courtesy and hospitality, especially Colonel Charles A. Brown and his staff, including Sergeant I. G. Edmonds; to the Customer Relations division of North American Aviation, Inc., specifically Earl Blount, Al Smith, and Edward Jacoby; to Edward H. Kolcum of NASA; and last but not least my gratitude for the friendly hospitality extended me in Los Angeles by Forrest J. Ackerman, and Vivian and John D. K. Brunner.

CONTENTS

1. *On the Mojave Desert* 9
2. *The Unfalling Golf Ball* 17
3. *Flight Test Center* 24
4. *Rocket Ship X-15* 29
5. *Under the Evening Star* 35
6. *Practice Makes Perfect* 41
7. *Seven-Day Deadline* 47
8. *Space Suit for One* 52
9. *Landing Pattern* 57
10. *Spaceman's Initials* 65
11. *Chariot for a High-Flier* 70
12. *Action Stations* 76
13. *The Tracker* 82
14. *The Missing Astronaut* 90
15. *Missile Cargo* 95
16. *X-15 Countdown* 102
17. *On the Warpath* 109
18. *The Stars by Day* 115
19. *Sidewinder Justice* 122

CHAPTER 1

ON THE MOJAVE DESERT

EDGING up to the mountains which rim the great city of Los Angeles to the east is one of the most inhospitable deserts of North America, the barren Mojave. Its waterless sandy wastes stretch out for hundreds of miles and form part of what the pioneers of the old frontier days called the Great American Desert. It covers most of several states, and of its many regions, the Mojave, high in altitude, freezing at night and burning by day, has the worst reputation. Rising high towards the bare peaks to its west it dips gradually down into the terrible depression known as Death Valley.

Lying close to the western edge of that terrifying desert is another strange and mysterious place, this one made by man. It is a place of long runways and low wide buildings, of strange metal towers and a self-contained secretive township spread out over the sands alongside the hard flat bottom of a dried-up lake.

Whereas nothing normally breaks the silence of the Mojave save the hiss of a snake, the dry scraping of a scorpion, and the eerie howl of a hungry coyote, this settlement is the scene of ear-shattering roars and ground-shaking rumbles. Now and again, from the low hills bordering Edwards Air Force Base, which is the settlement's name, comes the raging, roaring sound of mighty rocket engines, blasting away on captive test stands. Again and more often, there is the angry full-throated bellowing of jet engines undergoing ground examination. Almost always, somewhere in the clear skies there will be the beat and throb of fast powerful planes roaring and racing around, raging upwards, streaking back again. Their white jet trails cross and crisscross the blue heavens, but on the ground, busy men in overalls and in Air Force uniforms scarcely bother to look up from their own work.

For it is here that the work of the conquest of the air is being completed and much of the work for the conquest of space is being started, And it was at this place of secret mis-

EDWARDS AIR BASE

This is the scene of ear-shattering roars.

sions and world-shaking projects one morning in April that a stranger arrived.

He had driven in by car and apparently was familiar with the place for he had managed to avoid any official inspection or questioning. He had driven directly to the visitors' quarters and had there registered for a room.

He was a man with gaunt features, a thin-lipped unsmiling expression, and a small hooked scar over one cheek. When asked to fill out the registration for his billeting, he put down the name Carl Cahoon, which was not his real name, and when asked to state his business at the base he claimed to be an engineer called in for consultation at one of the airplane corporations located there. This also was not the truth, but no one thought to check on this for indeed a great many engineers and civilian experts came and went at the Air Force Flight Test Center.

Once he had settled himself in his room in the quadrangle of buildings set aside for unmarried officers and legitimate visitors, he took out a map of the base and studied it carefully. He noted the location of a certain hangar, and checked the roads leading to it. Satisfied, he left his room, carefully locking the door and made his way to his car.

He drove to a public telephone booth located in the shopping center of the enlisted men's quarters and there he put in a long distance phone call.

"Harger?" he said when he had made his connection. "You know who this is. Call me Cahoon here. I'm at the base, as you planned."

"Good," said the voice at the other end, that of the father of the astronaut, Rod Harger. The senior Harger was a man with plans for his son that did not include the ideals that dominate the Air Force and that had little to do with patriotism or love of country. Harger loved himself, and he loved money and fame. Fame, in fact, meant money. He had made his own fortune in shady dealing during the Second World War when he had shirked his own military duties to line his pockets at the expense of his fellow soldiers. He saw his son's selection as a space flier as a great opportunity and he wasn't going to let a few things like fair play and an officer's honor stand in his way.

"Get the dope on this X-15 flight plan," went on Harger's voice. "If anyone's going to take that up successfully, it's got to be Rod. I don't want any slip-ups on this."

"Don't worry," said Cahoon. "I'll keep my hand in, and things are going to work out right this time. I aim to keep my eye on that Mike Mars and his redskin friend too. They're a pair I've got a personal reason to get back at. Especially that Mars guy. Him I'm going to fix, but good!"

"Uh-uh," said Harger Senior. "Don't let your personal grudge get in the way of this operation. That's not what I'm paying you for."

"Never mind that, boss," said Cahoon sharply. "I'll do your work, but that kid Mars tried to kill me with his jet plane when he forced me down. I darned near could have broken my neck when I crashed and I only just got away from the state troopers by the skin of my teeth. I got a debt to pay him. Nobody does me dirt and gets away with it!"

"Now listen," said Harger sharply. "Just watch your step this time. And get in touch with Rod too. He ought to know what's going on."

"O.K.," said the gaunt man, "I'll get on the job. You'll be hearing from me."

Hanging up, he left the booth with the sort of smile on his face that a snake might have when sighting a nest of helpless young chicks.

It was on that same day, quite late in the afternoon, that the young astronaut Cahoon had mentioned, Mike Mars, was being driven along one of the roads leading to the experimental hangars. He was jammed into the front seat of a little red car alongside his fellow astronaut, Johnny Bluehawk. The car was being driven by its owner, the famous test pilot Kent Scott. Kent drove with the same skill and speed that characterized his flying.

Mike and Johnny had already had a busy day but they were both excited. For Kent was taking them to get a first look at the plane which might well be the world's first real spaceship, the famous rocket plane, X-15.

"That X-15's a tricky one to fly," Scott said as he steered. "I'll warn you right now you got to keep your wits about you. Rockets are a lot more powerful than even the fast jets you boys have learned to handle. You want to study everything about this plane before you try to take her up."

"I've been thinking of flying rockets since I was a kid in junior high," Mike answered. "There's nothing I'd rather learn than that. After all, it's the only road to space flight."

Scott shook his head. "You don't want to think too much

about space flight, kid," he said, deftly turning the car into the narrow road leading to the low aluminum-painted building that housed North American's works. "When you've been handling experimental planes as long as I have, you got to take things as they come. Get on top of what you have to work with and don't think about what's coming next. Look on this as a plane that's mean and hard to handle. Never mind the space angle."

Mike laughed. "Well, that's a safe viewpoint, but I can't help it. I'm living for the day I get out there among the stars."

"That's for me, too," said Johnny Bluehawk. "I'm going to shoot an arrow beyond the air—and where it lands, I'll be there."

"Hey," said Scott. "An Indian poet! But here we are. All out."

The three pushed out of the little car and stretched their cramped legs. They stood in front of the main entrance to the plant. They went over to the doors, and Scott hammered on the glass panel to be let in.

Looking through the glass they could see a light over the reception desk inside but nobody in sight. "After hours these places are deserted," Scott said. "The guard should be expecting us though."

He knocked again. Still nobody in sight. He tried the door and found it open. "Maybe he hasn't locked up yet," said Mike.

The three went into the silent building. They went up to the desk at which all visitors had to register and all employees had to check in. There was no one there.

"That's strange," said Kent Scott. "I spoke to O'Shaugnessy just a few minutes ago and he said he'd be here."

He looked down the dark hall with the several closed doors prominently marked with *No Admittance* signs. Mike looked around too. Johnny Bluehawk stood there before the desk silent and concentrating. Then he put his hands on the counter top and lightly vaulted over.

No sooner had he alighted on the other side than he gave out a whistle. "Look here!"

The other two quickly ran around. A man lay crumpled on the floor behind the desk. He was wearing a gray private watchman's uniform and lay sprawled face down as if asleep. The three squatted down over him, and Scott lifted his head.

"He's breathing," Scott said in a relieved tone. "But somebody's slipped up on him and knocked him over the head. He's been knocked out."

Mike stood up sharply. "That must have been only a couple of minutes ago then. Whoever did it must still be in the building!"

Johnny came to his feet with him. The two dashed quickly around the desk, raced down the hall. They guessed right for the third door they came to was not closed. It was ajar. With Scott pounding on their heels, they shoved it open and ran through it.

They came up with a bang in a shadowy vastness. They were in the hangar itself. Dim light of late afternoon came through wide windows set high up in the walls. Before them they could see the pointed nose and narrow dark shape of a long strange airplane. Beyond that further back in the dim hangar were two more similar shapes, and further on a more standard type of airplane.

But their eyes were not on the X-15 although it was what they came to see. Their eyes were caught by something moving behind the second of the three bulletlike vessels.

"Stop, you!" shouted Mike and started running toward the intruder.

There was a whispered curse and the unknown, bent low,

ran back into the depths of the hangar. Mike and Johnny, with Scott trailing them, charged after him, dodging around the planes, trying to catch the man.

As he ran through the confusing shadows of the unfamiliar hangar Mike saw that the man was trying to reach a door at the far end. And just as Mike was thinking that before the man would get that door unbolted he'd be on top of him, his leg caught in a trailing wire running along the ground where some workman had rigged up a temporary line.

Mike went sprawling, landing on his hands and knees. Before he could get to his feet again, Johnny came pell-mell into him and hit the ground in a jumble of arms. Scott, pounding on Johnny's heels, tried to jump aside, caught his foot in another strand of the wire and went down in a heap of his own.

By the time the three had unscrambled themselves and got to their feet, the far hangar door was open and the fading light of the afternoon streaming in. There was no sign of the stranger.

They reached the door, but whoever it was had made good his escape.

The unknown ran back into the hangar.

CHAPTER 2

THE UNFALLING GOLF BALL

EARLIER that day Johnny Bluehawk's sharp black eyes were fixed on a golf ball hanging from a string. Or rather, as he noted, it was not quite dangling. The string in fact was quite

Johnny's eyes were fixed on a golf ball.

slack, it had a bend in it, and the golf ball was simply hanging there as if entirely uninterested in falling down properly and making the string taut.

Now anywhere else on Earth this would have been a very surprising thing, but not here. In fact Johnny would have been quite upset if it hadn't been so limply defying gravity. That was the way things should be at this particular place and time.

The place was about 30,000 feet up in the clear Southern California air. The time was a few seconds after Johnny had pulled the long speedy F-100F jet fighter plane up into the long parabolic curve that would create the rare condition of zero gravity—the condition where the forces of inertia and centrifugal drive exactly countered the drag of the Earth's gravitation.

This was the second such curve he had run on this flight and behind him he could hear through the earphones of his flying helmet the breathing of his fellow astronaut, Mike Mars. This was Mike Mars' show at the moment—Johnny had already run through his own the day before when Mike had been the pilot in the front seat and the young Cheyenne the passenger going through the tests.

Now it was Mike in the back seat, wearing a Navy Mark 4 pressure suit tightly encasing his body against the dangers of a sudden loss of pressure. Apparently Mike was not expecting such a loss for beneath the pressurized protection of the tightly sealed transparent canopy that closed in the two-seater jet, he had the face plate of his helmet open and was reaching for something on the rack of objects banked before his seat.

His gray eyes twinkled and his freckled features cracked as he spoke softly into his chest mike. "Feeling hungry, Johnny? Sorry, I can't offer you any, but I'm going to have a bite."

"I'm going to have a bite," Mike said.

In his earphones came the soft chuckle of his friend and fellow space-flying trainee, "Thanks, not right now. I've had mine. If you sink your teeth in that, you're a miracle worker."

"Oh?" Mike's eyes arched. He was not exactly resting in his seat for, though he was strapped, it was evident that he was exerting no pressure on the cushioned seat. In a condition of zero gravity, if he unstrapped himself and kicked a little, he could float about the narrow confines at will. This kind of demonstration was not however the purpose of the present experiment.

In his hand he now held what looked like a remarkable large toothpaste tube. He unscrewed the cap, held the tube to his lips, and gently squeezed it. Under the pressure of his fingers something brownish and thick flowed out into his opened mouth. He closed his teeth, tossed the mushy stuff around a bit, and swallowed by a conscious effort.

"Mmmm," he said, "good. Chopped beef. Goes down all right too."

The helmeted head in the seat ahead of him, visible to Mike as only the top of a helmet from one side of which a little blue feather stuck up jauntily, nodded. Mike tried another mouthful of the food. "Goes down all right," he remarked.

Another voice cut into his headphones. "Take a drink of water now, and see how it goes." The voice had a strong German accent and belonged to Dr. Hugo Holderlin of the School of Aviation Medicine. Dr. Holderlin was not in the plane. He was down on the ground, but he was directly connected with the highflying jet and not a thing went on in that plane that he did not know of.

"O.K., doc," said Mike and reached for another container. This one was a sort of squirt bottle, like a plastic catsup container. Holding this to his face, he pressed. Immediately a little jet of water streamed out. It missed his mouth at first, and bounced off his face.

Mike bobbed his head around and even as the little drops of water were forming into tiny beads floating around in space on their own, not falling to the floor, he rounded them up with his lips and swallowed.

"A near miss," he murmured, and he could hear the chuckle that came from the front seat.

"Very good," said Dr. Holderlin's voice. "Does it swallow all right?"

"No trouble at all," said Mike.

Johnny Bluehawk's voice cut in. "Get ready. We're coming out of it."

"I guess we'll be able to feed ourselves in outer space, anyway," said Mike.

"Just wait and see if you hold it down," came the words of the doctor who was monitoring the whole experiment from the ground.

Then with abrupt suddenness the situation inside the silvery plane changed. One second both pilot and his passenger had been floating lightly in their seats, the first intent on keeping the plane delicately adjusted to maintain that golf ball in its weightless float, the other intent on his experiment in feeding himself as he would have to when he got out into the eternal zero gravity of the space between the planets.

But now the plane had reached the farthest run of its wide curve and abruptly the young pilot pulled its nose upward, rammed up his jets and roared for the sky. Both of the pressure-suited riders felt themselves thrust hard back into their seats. The belts that restrained them clasped them with strong grips, the golf ball pulled down hard on its string, and the force of three times the normal pull of gravity placed its heavy hand on the plane and all within it.

In the back seat, the helmet of the young man, while the regulation Air Force helmet for this type of flying, bore upon its front the initials M.A.R.S. These were the initials of the young astronaut known to his friends as Mike Mars, but known officially on the records of Project Quicksilver as Michael Alfred Robert Samson, lieutenant in the United States Air Force.

Mike and his pilot, the young Cheyenne Johnny Bluehawk who had won his wings in the USAF side by side with Mike, were on the last series of a group of astronautic tests on the effects of zero gravity on space fliers. They had each performed a dozen such flights in the past week while the effects were carefully recorded by means of elaborate instruments attached to their bodies and to the plane. Mike's heartbeat, his breathing, and his blood pressure, all three were of intense interest to the problem of safety and life in outer space.

This, one of the last of the series, was to determine the effects of eating and drinking on a body without weight. Now you might suppose that food would not stay down if it didn't have any weight. Perhaps you might think that a person could chew it, try to swallow it, and then it wouldn't fall down his throat because it wouldn't have gravity to pull it down. Fortunately for us, gravity has nothing at all to do with eating.

Doctors have known a long time that food goes down one's gullet into the stomach—and through the digestive system after that—not because it is falling down of its own accord but because strong muscles lining the passages of the gullet, stomach, and intestines are forcing it along. The position of the body has nothing to do with it, as you can find out for yourself. Anybody who has tried to eat a piece of cake while lying on his back, or even hanging head down from the edge of a bed can prove to himself that it will get to the stomach even when actually traveling upward to do it!

So the fact that the ground meat in that plastic tube could feed a spaceman in space was not a surprise to Mike Mars. What the test really was to show was whether the fact that Mike himself had no weight would have a bad effect afterwards. Maybe Mike's internal muscles would get mixed up because of the unaccustomed loss of weight. Or maybe Mike would feel nauseous because of the strange condition—a condition never found normally on the surface of the Earth save for a second or two when you jump off a diving board!

But so far it seemed all right.

For the next minute Mike and his pilot endured the burden of triple gravity acceleration. This was not just an accident of the flight, for it too was deliberate. After zero gravity, Dr. Holderlin wanted to know how well the body would react to a heavy demand on its muscles. In space a pilot might be required suddenly to ram on his rockets, move speedily. If such a change was to have bad effects, it would be better to find out before building spaceships.

"How's it going, Mike?" came Johnny's voice, forced through straining lips and tensed muscles.

Mike was engaged in attempting to put some pegs into a board which had holes especially prepared for it. He was concentrating on it, his hands forcing themselves against the heavy strain of the rising plane.

"Coming along all right," he spoke softly, mouthing each word before forcing it out. "This is pie."

Then the plane leveled off and the pressure was over. Both young fellows relaxed.

Dr. Holderlin's voice came over their phones. "Bring her down now," he said. "We have a conference coming yet this afternoon."

"O.K.," said Johnny. "Here goes."

The sleek roaring plane swung wide, performed a wide circle

over the yellowish-brown desert that lay far below them. Behind the F-100F a line of puffy white smoke appeared, the control of the jet, and made a slender white line in the clear cold air.

Deftly the young Indian brought the plane closer, swung it down, called to the tower for instructions, and then came swinging low over the buildings and hangars.

Mike looked down, taking advantage of the leisure of being a passenger for once. As Johnny swung the ship low over one of the far hangars set up around the far-flung base, he squinted his eyes sharply.

"Hey," he called, "that looks like the X-15 out there. See it, Johnny? The dark bullet-nosed ship just outside behind that hangar?"

Johnny glanced down. He swung the fast jet around, roared low over the hangar in question, craning his neck as he passed.

"Sure thing," he said as they passed over it. "That's the X-15 rocket ship itself." He drew back his head, concentrating on his landing.

Mike looked back. "Gosh," he said, "how I'd like to get a ride in that. That's a real spaceship, it really is."

Dr. Holderlin's voice cut in dryly, for he had not cut off his communication with them. "Bring the ship in, boys. You can get a better look at the X-15 from the ground, if you stop wasting time sky-rubber-necking."

"Yippee!" said the two simultaneously as the wheels of the F-100F bounced on the far end of the runway and the drag parachute popped out to bring their ship to a halt.

X15

CHAPTER 3

FLIGHT TEST CENTER

JOHNNY taxied the sleek silvery Super Sabre down the runway and up to the base operations building at the field. As he did so, Mike had slid back the transparent canopy that shielded the two and was looking out over the landscape. "This is sure one of the longest runways I've ever seen," he commented as the ship came to a halt and the whine of its jet ceased.

"I guess they had plenty of space out here in the Mojave Desert for it," said Johnny unstrapping himself and preparing to climb out as the ground crew came racing up to meet them.

"Besides," said Mike, "since the purpose of this base is to test experimental planes, I guess they need the extra space. Some of these tricky jobs may balk or even fail to get off the first time."

They climbed out. Gray-haired Dr. Hugo Holderlin, one of the famous German rocket scientists who was now a leader in the field of space medicine, met them on the ground. Even as the two young pilots walked to the base operations building to remove their cumbersome flying equipment, he was busy querying Mike about the tests. This was standard practice at all such experiments. There were often little things that would be forgotten minutes after the test was over—and these little things might be important clues as to how man would act when out in the weightlessness of space.

Every man being tested was quizzed as soon as he landed. Of course Mike also knew that everything physical had been recorded by the instruments even while it was going on. But often, as the doctor had pointed out, there were things like the state of a man's mind and his emotional feelings that played a part.

"You know," Dr. Holderlin said, "when you go out into space, you cannot just sit down and eat a meal when you are hungry. Nothing has weight, so nothing stays on the plate. You reach for a potato—ach! It floats away like a toy balloon. You cut the meat; the piece you cut off slides away and heads for the wall. You want a glass of water, you pick it up, the glass stops in your hand, the water keeps on going up, forming a ball until it hits the ceiling, bounces off into a thousand little balls and floats all around the room."

Mike laughed. "I could see that even in the minute up there. So that's why the food comes ground up in a plastic tube?"

"Ja," said the doctor. "That's one way of doing it. But at least you can get the food into your mouth that way. We are working constantly on this problem of feeding men in space. Tell me, it feels all right? You're not a little sick, maybe from eating without weight?"

"No, not me," said Mike. "In fact I'm still a little hungry."

"That's good," said the doctor. "It's a matter of the mind too. You know, sometimes if the man is just a little scared about the flight, maybe a little nervous, he gets sick quicker."

Johnny Bluehawk laughed then. "Not Mike here. He's been

Johnny Bluehawk

so anxious to get to Mars, I think he's happier up there than here."

They checked in their stuff and joined the doctor in a staff car outside. They drove silently along the road winding from the main air fields to the big blue building that housed the National Aeronautics and Space Administration staff at the Air Force Flight Test Center.

They entered the NASA building, rode up to their floor, followed Dr. Holderlin to the rooms that had been set aside for their use. On the door of the main room, as they pushed it open, was pinned a temporary sign. It read, *Space Task Group Q*.

That was Project Quicksilver.

As they entered the little conference room, there were four others waiting for them. One was Colonel Drummond, head of Space Task Group Q, their commander and director. Another, a slim dark-haired man in civilian dress, possibly in his thirties, was a stranger to Mike. The other two were not. They, too, were astronauts.

One was Jack Lannigan, lanky Navy pilot, who had become a close friend of Mike and Johnny's during the difficult tests of the past months. They had been among the seven chosen for space-flight training. The other was Rod Harger, Jr.

Rod, chunky, cold-eyed, straw-haired pilot, had originally come from the same training school as Mike, had even been on Mike's flying team. But it could not be said that the two had ever become chums. Rod was not given to close friendships; he had a different viewpoint on the work they were doing than the others, though he kept that view to himself and to those who secretly worked with him.

Mike and the others looked on space flight as the greatest achievement of humanity. They regarded it as the biggest step to human advancement, as the opening of a new and endless frontier that would benefit everyone. For them it was the achievement which was important, which was bigger than their personal futures.

Rod saw it differently. For him, space flight was just a means to make himself rich and famous. He wanted to be first in space, because he wanted the glory and the rewards that would come with it. He cared nothing about what it might mean to the rest of his country or the rest of the world.

It would be fun to be the first man in space, Mike knew, and Lannigan knew, and Johnny Bluehawk, and the three other members of thier team who were working on different tests elsewhere would have agreed. But it was not important enough to make a man sulk if one of his friends made it instead. It was the team that counted, they all thought.

Of course, Rod never let on as to his private thoughts. If he had, it would have hurt his game.

Mike and Johnny greeted the others and exchanged some bantering on the test flights. The others had completed their series of zero gravity flights already. The newcomers drew up chairs.

The colonel cleared his throat. "Fellows," he began, "you've all come through those tests very well, I'm glad to say. None of you has shown any ill effects from zero gravity, and you've all adjusted well to the various problems presented under those conditions. Of course, even sixty seconds of weightless conditioning are not really enough to know how a human body would react under sixty minutes or sixty hours of it—but we think the tests begin to give us at least some start on the problem. We'll never know how longer periods work out until we actually go into space." He paused dramatically, then said, "And that may be sooner than we expect."

The four astronauts drew in their breaths. The colonel turned to the dark-haired stranger. "I don't know if you have recognized our visitor from his picture, but if you haven't let me introduce him. This is Kent Scott, who has been one of the test pilots of the X-15."

There was a pause. The colonel took a breath, then announced dramatically. "I can now inform you that this remarkable plane has been officially turned over to the Air Force by its builders. The next flights of the X-15 will be under our control, and specifically under the control of Space Task Group Q. In short, you fellows are going to learn to fly this rocket ship, the first space-going plane ever produced!"

"This is Kent Scott."

CHAPTER 4

ROCKET SHIP X-15

"You know," said Colonel Drummond, "when we were first selecting men for our project I pointed out that it was a younger group than the Project Mercury Astronauts. Some of us at NASA felt that we needed to train very young men for space, young pilots with quick youthful muscles and minds and without family ties. We felt that it would be the younger men who would grow up with the science of space flight, and who would not be too old to fly to the Moon and the planets when the rockets are perfected.

"So we got permission to start a second space training group and that we called Project Quicksilver."

He looked at each of them, dwelling a little bit on Rod Harger. "Some of you have wondered why you have not received the publicity that the Mercury Astronauts have had. You are getting much the same training. Your program for space flight is very nearly the same. Nobody has interviewed you for the newspapers. Nobody has published your pictures in the magazines. Nobody has even asked you what kind of chewing gum you chew or what pretty actress you like to watch best in the movies.

"In fact, you have been kept quite secret. You have been told to keep everything hush-hush and nobody even knows there is a Project Quicksilver Astronaut group, whereas everybody knows all about the Mercury men."

Mike nodded and glanced at the others. This was true, but he hadn't personally thought much about it. He'd been much too busy.

All his life Michael Alfred Robert Samson had wanted to fly to Mars. He'd been in the habit of putting his initials, M.A.R.S., on everything beginning with his schools books, his baseball bat and everything else. He'd earned the nickname of Mike Mars from that, and it had stuck even when he'd joined the Air Force and had gone through the hard studies and discipline of learning to be a jet plane pilot.

When he'd been selected as one of the seven very young

new pilots to be an astronaut, it had been but the start of an exciting series of new studies and tests. He'd spent the first two months at Langley Field, in Virginia, studying the basic problems of space flight. There'd been a heavy and full schedule there.

He'd studied astronomy and the planets all over again. He'd refreshed his knowledge of meteorology. He'd worked on the mathematics and technology of rocketry, the operations of

Mike Mars

recoil and reaction engines. He'd been kept active with a series of physical tests, designed to keep him and the others in topnotch condition. He'd ridden the G-force centrifuge many times, building up his resistance to heavy strains and the pressure of quick acceleration, which would surely be a condition of rocket flight.

Then had come a series of visits to other places, further investigations into the space flight studies, and now here at the

Air Force Flight Test Center he'd just completed another series of such workouts. He'd had no time to wonder why nobody had given him publicity.

It had just never occurred to him. He was too busy learning to be a space flier to worry about his picture in the paper. Yet, what the colonel had said had been true. Why?

"Our Project Mercury Astronauts represent the officially acknowledged program for placing a man in space. But as you know we are in a race with another great world power, one that has made some big jumps into space that has caused many people to believe it to be ahead of our country. If we were to take the risks openly that this power must have taken to get there, there would be too much public protest, too many claims that we were heedless of life.

"Now as you know from your own experience, we are not at all reckless with life. But there are certain advantages in keeping many of our experiments and progress secret.

"We are not going to show all our cards just to boast. We are really going to blast ahead with a secret group of astronauts that nobody will know about. Those men are you."

The colonel paused, looked around at the intent serious faces watching him. Mike found himself leaning forward, caught in the dramatic thought of what he was taking part in.

"You men are our secret weapon. Without family ties, young and daring, ready for risks that cautious and older test pilots would not undertake, you are going to be moved ahead secretly and the world is not going to hear of you until you have planted Old Glory on the Moon. Then and only then will we admit the existence of Project Quicksilver."

The colonel stopped, sat back in his chair. The others relaxed, looked around at each other, wrapped for a while in their own thoughts. They had all had some suspicion of this, but they had never brought the thought out as clearly.

Now Colonel Drummond turned to the serious-faced test pilot, Kent Scott. He nodded to him. Scott glanced around at the four young pilots until he saw he had their attention. He spoke in a soft calm voice:

"I've been asked to brief you on the X-15. You surely all know a little about it, and I'm not going into the details of its construction now because you're going to have plenty of time to study for yourselves on the real thing. I'll just tell you how it came about.

"Way back in 1954, NASA assigned a team to study the

problem of building a plane capable of flight beyond the atmosphere for the purpose of exploring conditions in space. This plane had to be one that could be manned, could be

"I've been asked to brief you on the X-15."

guided by its pilot, could return in one piece and land safely.

"Now the X-15 is not the first plane to use rockets as its power source. Yet as you realize only a rocket-driven plane could fulfill the conditions of being able to navigate in airless space. The jets and turbojets all require the presence of air in order to function. But a rocket carries its own oxygen as part of its fuel and is independent of air.

"The X-15 is designed to fly in outer space. It has been tested several times here at Edwards, the first independent glide flight and landing having been made on June 8, 1959. It is now ready for man's first drive beyond the borders of the atmosphere."

Scott picked up a sheaf of papers and folders and passed them out to the boys. "You'll find the data on the X-15 given here. Study it, read up on it, and tomorrow we will begin work on learning how the X-15 is constructed and how it is to be flown."

He looked at his watch, turned to the colonel. "I guess it's time to knock off. It's past closing time at the maintenance building, and will be time for chow in another hour."

Mike glanced up from the papers he'd been scanning. "Excuse me," he said. "I did catch sight of the X-15 out back of its hangar. Maybe it would be possible, right now, just to go over and have a quick look at it, for a minute or two."

Johnny joined him. "That would be good," he said. "I'd like to see it too."

Scott scratched his head. "Well, I guess you could still see it, in spite of the hour. Hold on, I'll call the place and see if anyone's around."

"I think we can wait till tomorrow morning," said Rod Harger coolly. "Really it's silly to rush out for just a glimpse."

"It's no trouble," said Scott. He went to the phone on a nearby desk, dialed a number. There was a wait, then an answer.

"O'Shaugnessy? . . . This is Scott, Kent Scott. Is anybody there who can give some pilots a quick look at the X-15? . . . The engineers have all gone home? . . . Uh, huh . . . You will? Good. O.K., these fellows will be over in about fifteen minutes. I'll bring them. See you."

Scott hung up, turned. "The hangar's closed for the day, but O'Shaugnessy's the security officer on duty tonight and he'll let us in if we don't delay. Who's coming?"

Mike jumped up. "I'm coming." Johnny stood up, reached for his hat. "Me too."

Lannigan shook his head. "I can't make it tonight. I'll just have to wait."

Harger stood up, shrugged his shoulders. "Tomorrow for me. I'll study these papers first, then I'll know what I'm looking at."

"Me, I can't wait," said Mike. "A real spaceship is something I've wanted to see a long time." He followed Scott and Johnny Bluehawk out, humming an excited little tune as he went.

CHAPTER 5

UNDER THE EVENING STAR

HAVING missed the prowler the three shut and bolted the hangar door and made their way back through the shadowy interior, being careful this time to watch out for wires strewn along the floor. Back near the first of the X-15 models, they stopped.

Kent Scott said, "Wait here, but don't touch anything. I'm going to see if I can bring O'Shaugnessy to, and then I'll have to call in the Air Force police."

The two astronauts stood by the corridor door and looked silently at the bulk of the rocket ships. They could hear Scott's voice down the hall, first trying to arouse the guard, then talking on the phone.

In a few minutes they heard him coming back, accompanied by another hesitant tread. Scott returned to the inner hangar half-supporting the guard, now conscious and holding his head.

"Did he damage anythin'?" said the guard in a slow and still weak tone.

"I don't think he had time," said Scott, "but we'll have to have everything carefully checked tomorrow morning. Did you see him at all?"

"That I did not," said the guard straightening up a little and apparently regaining something of his breath. "I was seated at the desk there, making a note of the time and your call about coming in, when I had the feeling that someone was near me. I started to look up and—*bang*—I saw stars, I did, and just went down for the count. He must have hit me with a pipe he must have. Slipped in somewhere—we'll have to look for how he did that—and conked me proper."

"He might have come in by the same outside door that he left by," put in Mike. "He knew where to run when we broke in."

"I guess he could that," said O'Shaugnessy. "Possibly he sneaked in while the place was open and hid till the men had left. It couldn't be easy, but I suppose it could happen."

"The police must be coming now," said Scott, "I hear cars pulling up." The four of them made their way to the main entrance where indeed a squad of helmeted and armed Air Force police were piling in the door.

After the situation had been explained and the boys described what had happened, Scott drew the two aside. "We'd better go. There's not going to be time for looking over the X-15 today any more. Besides, I'm hungry."

"He conked me proper!"

So the three got back into Scott's car and drove back to their quarters. As they drove, Mike thought of something.

"I'm sort of surprised to find there are three X-15s," he remarked. "You know everyone speaks of the plane as if it was just one, the X-15. But there are three of them in that hangar all alike."

Scott laughed. "Now you don't suppose we'd spend all that money and research just to make one plane—and then have the plane blow up or be destroyed in a crash while testing it? That would be too great a risk.

"We built three copies of the plane, so that whatever happens to the one being tested, what we learn can be corrected and put into the other two that are still safe on the ground. That's the way all experimental new planes are built—you always make three of them."

The only trouble with that, Mike thought, was that if the X-15 were to crash when he flew it, they might have two others around—but how many Mike Marses were there? And, of course, his mind answered his own question. There were six other astronauts. Still . . . it didn't seem like quite the same thing.

Back at quarters, Mike and Johnny washed up, banged on Rod and Jack Lannigan's doors, and when the other two astronauts joined them, went out and had dinner. The other two hadn't heard what had happened and both seemed quite disturbed. Rod, for some reason, looked quite uneasy about it.

Lately Rod had seemed more like one of the fellows. In fact he seemed a lot easier to get along with, as if somehow having been selected as one of the seven he had got over a hurdle that meant more to him than perhaps it should have. Mike didn't quite fully warm up to him, but he had learned early that it is better to try to get along than to show your dislike and make an outright enemy. Mike, by nature, always felt that the other fellow deserved a break, and should get the benefit of any doubt. Mike wanted to win, just as any young fellow wants to win, but he wanted to win fair.

"What I don't understand," said Jack Lannigan, "is what did the intruder want? If he was a spy for some foreign power, he certainly didn't allow himself enough time to learn anything much. If he wanted to sabotage the planes, that would be silly because these planes are always carefully checked out before any flight. No sabotage done in haste would escape detection."

"Maybe he just wanted to get the layout, just to sort of size the situation up for future sabotage," said Mike. "You know—briefing himself on possibilities."

They chewed on that in silence. Finally Jack said, "That could mean that we ought to look out for a real serious attempt later on. We'll have to master not only the X-15 itself, and that won't be easy, but also keep our eyes open for trouble that isn't connected with the plane's own crankiness."

"Yes," Mike said to that, drinking the last of the milk he preferred to coffee, "and that means that we'd better get back to our rooms and get to work on those papers. So we'll be ready to really start studying the X-15 itself tomorrow."

Agreeing, the others drew away from the table, and walked back slowly to their quarters. They walked in gathering twilight over the sandy wastes that was the Mojave Desert across which the base sprawled. Underfoot the rough sand and gravel crunched, and in the darkening sky the first gleam shone, the white steady dot that was the Evening Star, the planet Venus.

Mike looked up at it as he walked, and called it to the attention of the others. "There she is," he said softly. "That's one of our targets. Always popping up first to keep us reminded that we're not alone in the universe. Strange mysterious Venus, planet of eternal clouds. Target number two, as I see it."

Rod Harger looked at it too. "The Moon is number one, Venus number two. I'd like to get to the Moon, but I don't know about the second target. Venus, some say, is a pretty deadly world. I hear the latest theory is that it's way above the boiling point of water on its surface. No place to land a spaceship."

Mike grunted. "Astronomers are always arguing about it. They used to think it had no water at all, but now that they've been able to take measurements from a stratosphere balloon they know it has water vapor. I think, in spite of the claims about its hot surface, that somehow we'll manage to land a ship on it. There may be high plateaus that are cooler, and in any case, the polar regions ought to be colder."

"Yeah," said Jack, "instead of boiling away at six hundred degrees you can fry comfortably at three hundred. I don't especially want to go to Venus either."

"Well," said Mike sharply, "I do. I'm game to find out. I have a firm belief that what the human mind can dream of, the human mind can find a way to do. I don't know how we can survive on Venus, but I'm sure that when the Air Force is ready to go there, they'll be prepared for it."

"That's so," said Johnny. "It's going to be a few years before we can even think seriously of it, and by that time we ought to know a good deal more about the problem than we do now. Besides there'll be Venus probe rockets very soon now."

"Uh-huh," said Mike. "I expect that any day—and before we even think of sending a man there, they'll know the real

Mike looked at the stranger.

facts about the planet's surface and its heat. Besides, first things first. We've got the X-15 to take up the first hundred miles."

"They say the first hundred miles are the hardest," commented Rod, with a slightly forced laugh.

They reached their building, went in, climbed the stairs to their floor. They broke up, going to their separate rooms to spend a few hours in study before going to bed. As Mike came to his door and opened it, he glanced down the long corridor. A man started to come out of a room down the long hall. For an instant Mike and the stranger looked at each other, and then the other turned and went back quickly into his room as if he had forgotten something.

Mike stepped into his own room, put on the light, closed the door. He was puzzled. For an instant he thought he had known that man, yet somehow he couldn't place him. A thin, gaunt face—now where had he seen that face before? The suggestion of a scar—or was it a scar? The man had been in shadow and distant.

Mike shrugged, thrust the teasing shadow of memory from his mind, and sat down to read through the basic papers on the rocket ship's construction.

CHAPTER 6

PRACTICE MAKES PERFECT

MIKE didn't have much time to spare to wonder about the identity of the prowler at the X-15 hangar. Nor did he have time to work on the tantalizing memory of the other stranger, the one whose face he had spotted in the hall of the visitors' quarters. For promptly the next morning he and his comrades were engaged in learning what made the X-15 tick, and how to master its controls.

The security men had searched the area of the prowler and had come up with nothing. There were no clues as to what he had wanted nor who he was nor where he had gone. The maintenance men had just about taken all three models of the X-15 apart trying to find some evidence of tampering, but they found nothing at all. It was apparent that the arrival of Scott and the two boys had prevented the prowler from achieving his objective. Thereafter the building was guarded by additional watchmen and no further effort was made to break in.

One result of the mysterious incident was the decision of Colonel Drummond to have the four astronauts issued side-arms—regulation revolvers. "Considering the attacks made on some of you when you were just Quicksilver candidates, then this, I think you should be armed for your own protection."

The four astronauts of Project Quicksilver gathered at the X-15 plant and began their studies. While the engineers were examining the planes for damage, they took advantage of the search to see the insides of the plane whose parts they had already studied in diagram.

The X-15 was a surprisingly small plane, as modern high-speed craft go. In length it was even a bit shorter than the F-100 jets that Mike was used to, for it was but fifty feet long from nose to tail, the Super Sabre being four feet longer. Narrower too, for its stubby wings, set far back to the rear, ran but twenty-two feet from tip to tip against the F-100's almost thirty-nine feet. It stood lower as well though since it had a different type of landing gear this could be discounted. But Mike couldn't help contrasting it in his mind and feeling that surely he could handle a little one like this, having mastered the powerful jet fighter.

He knew this thought was dangerously deceptive, and strove to put the impression out of his mind. The little blackish-brown, bullet-nosed ship was a rocket ship, and this made all the difference.

Rocket engines were far trickier, although in principle simpler, than the mighty jet-thrust drives of the Air Force fighters. The fuels to be burned in them were in themselves treacherous. The total time the engines could be in operation was far more limited, really fantastically slight, and yet the speed and force which the ship would attain in that limited time of operation would leave the best jet plane hopelessly out-distanced.

Mike had to learn to thrust aside what he knew about piloting a jet and start in to learn all over again what could be done with this terrific torpedo.

The first thing that impressed itself on his mind was how much of his time would be taken up with handling the X-15 as a glider. Looked at as such, he saw that its design resembled nothing so much as the streamlined paper darts that he used to make himself out of folded paper and shoot around classrooms during recess periods—that is, when he had nothing more important to do. As those paper darts, whose wings were thin tapering affairs folded back along the side, could skim through the air with speed, so also the X-15. Moving fast, the ship would glide effectively. Moved slowly, it could and would fall in a hopeless spiral plunge.

The entire X-15 was sheathed in an extremely hard and heat-resistant nickel alloy known as Inconel-X. In its tapering nose were four tiny compressed-air rocket tubes for use in directional navigation when out of the Earth's atmosphere. Here also were stored the landing wheels retracted when in flight. Just behind this space was the pilot's seat and the controls. A sloping narrow thickly protected window bulge came up here to allow the pilot forward and sideways vision. The pilot himself was cramped down in a specially built ejection seat with the controls so placed that they could be reached with the barest effort of the wrists. Just behind the pilot were the power units auxiliary and the helium tanks, followed by the storage tanks for liquid nitrogen and hydrogen peroxide

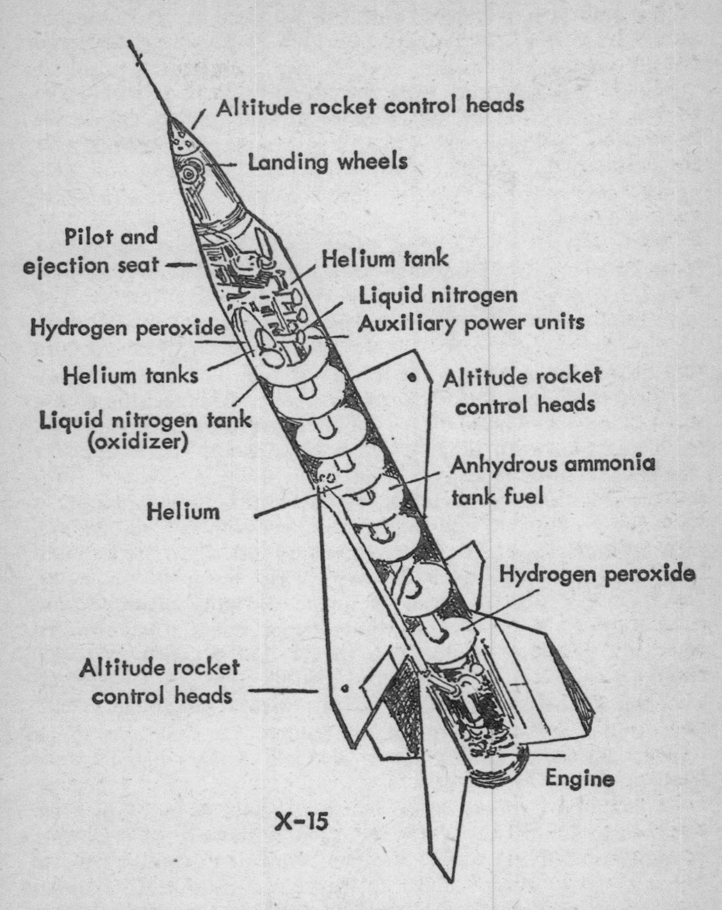

X-15

which were used for the X-15's unique cooling system, which would oppose the heating up of the body of the vessel and the pilot's space as well during the severe frictional strains of the plane's re-entry into the atmosphere.

Behind this area, which took barely more than the first third of the space, were the great tanks for the rocket fuels. The first was the tank for liquid oxygen, the second the tank for liquid ammonia, the latter quite the same as the stuff used by women for washing clothes. The liquid oxygen and the ammonia combine to make an explosive rocket fuel with the driving power necessary to do the job.

The last section of the plane was taken up by the engine itself. This followed, as all such engines do, the basic pattern of a combustion chamber where the fuels flowed in and were ignited and a nozzle from whence the fiery gases by escaping supplied the thrust.

Such was the X-15, and Mike and the other astronauts knew that just the knowledge of its outlines was not enough. For them it was but the beginning of the task. They worked side by side with the engineers who were tracing it and were putting it into shape for flight. They themselves attended to the fitting of the valves, the testing of the lines, the testing of feed tubes and indicators, the checking and rechecking of the tanks, and the wiring of the engine. For their problem, that of flying the craft, they would need to know this plane like the back of their hand.

The technique of mastering a new plane is the endless effort to achieve complete and total familiarity with it. One must be able to touch the right control almost by instinct at the moment that the brain first signals the need. This can only be done by practice, practice and more practice. But the problem here was that the X-15 was so highly experimental that none of the young fellows could hope to get that practice in actual flight.

Another method had been found to achieve familiarity with the X-15's controls. That was by means of a dummy cockpit with a complete dummy set of controls, exactly like those in the real thing.

This dummy cabin was set up on a centrifuge and in it Mike learned to control the X-15; facing its dashboard, dressed in a cumbersome flying suit to simulate the suit he would have to wear while in actual flight, he learned to fly the X-15 under conditions very much like those he would encounter in reality.

As the centrifuge whirled, the capsule containing Mike and the dummy controls rushing around the chamber at ever increasing speed, Mike could feel the pressure of acceleration on him, and could force himself to overcome the varying gravitation forces that would hamper his hands at their work.

Mike learned how to react immediately to the controls

Day after day he worked.

under any type of gravitational stress. The dashboard and its devices became, during the succeeding days, as familiar to him as his mother's face.

It was similar in most respects to the cockpit of the jet fighters he was used to. In the instrument panel there were dials registering speed, altitude, stability, rate of ascent or descent, and the performance of his engines.

To his left was the ballistic attitude control stick. A roll of his wrist or a thrust up and down or from side to side would fire the tiny rocket drives on the nose and the four set in the wings which would control the plane's position. Also to Mike's left would be the throttle that would control the master rocket drive.

To his right were the switches to control his communications, his navigational aids and his aerodynamic control stick, by means of which he could shift the surfaces of his wings and tails when gliding. These controls acted in concert with the standard central control stick, and were designed to be operated with just a slight wrist movement at times when the heavy pressure of acceleration would make moving the central stick too tedious a task.

Day after day, he worked, after spending time on the actual plane itself, until at last he felt himself completely at home, until the very effort of answering the message of his dials or the words on his earphones became a matter of split-second reaction.

It was only then that Mike Mars was ready for the next step in man's first visit to outer space.

CHAPTER 7

SEVEN-DAY DEADLINE

THERE was a meeting again in the same room in the NASA building as the one in which they had first been told of their new program. The four astronauts were there, as were their chiefs, Dr. Holderlin and Colonel Drummond. Present also was Kent Scott and three others. These three were briefly introduced to the rest. One was Major Coppard, who wore pilot's wings on his trim blue uniform. Another was an earnest young NASA engineer named Frank Moultrie, and the third a stocky quiet middle-aged civilian named Lentz, whom Mike remembered seeing around at the X-15 building and who turned out to be one of the chief construction engineers on that project.

The four astronauts shook hands with the newcomers, and relaxed in their seats. Lentz smiled at them. "I guess by now you are getting tired of make-believe flying. You must be pretty sick of dummy cockpits. Young fellows like you want to be up and going rather than playing with such toys."

Mike laughed. "Oh, I guess we can use our imaginations. Besides, I always was told by my mother that patience was a virtue."

"Patience, surely," said Colonel Drummond, "but even waiting has to have an end. Think you could fly the X-15 now?"

Mike and the three others felt themselves tightening up, but continued to keep their poise. "Well, sir," said Rod Harger quietly, "we've got all the necessary muscle reactions. My wrists twitch in my sleep."

Jack Lannigan guffawed. "Every night as soon as I close my eyes I imagine I'm in that cockpit. I'm flying all over the universe in it."

Johnny Bluehawk smiled and his dark black eyes crinkled, but he said nothing.

The colonel nodded. "We figured you were ready for the next step. Too much training can be as bad as too little. So

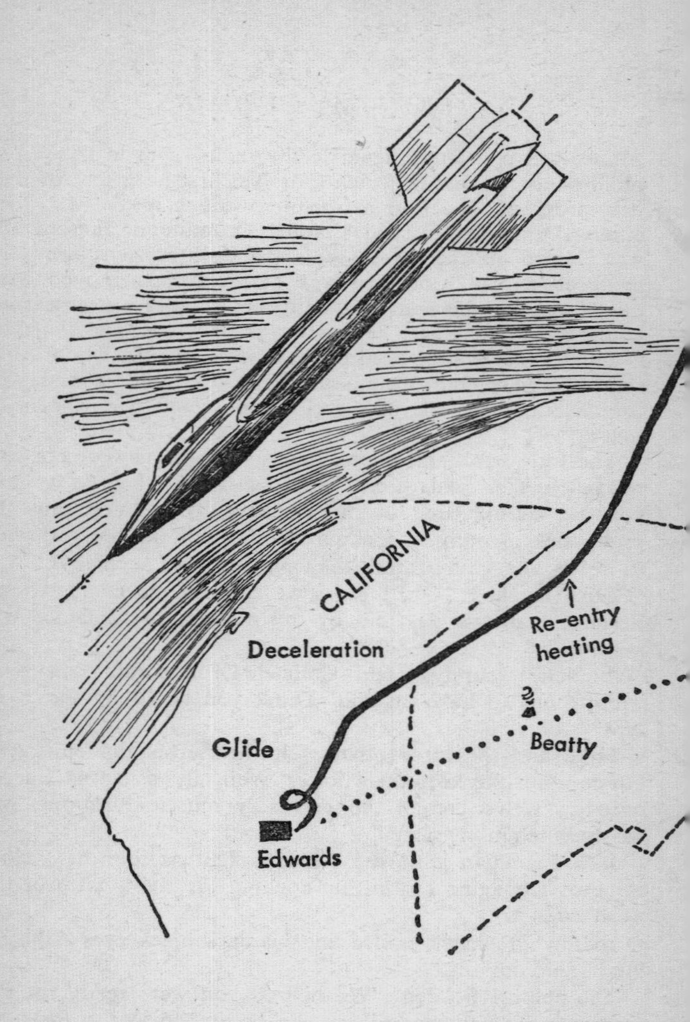
CALIFORNIA
Re-entry heating
Deceleration
Glide
Beatty
Edwards

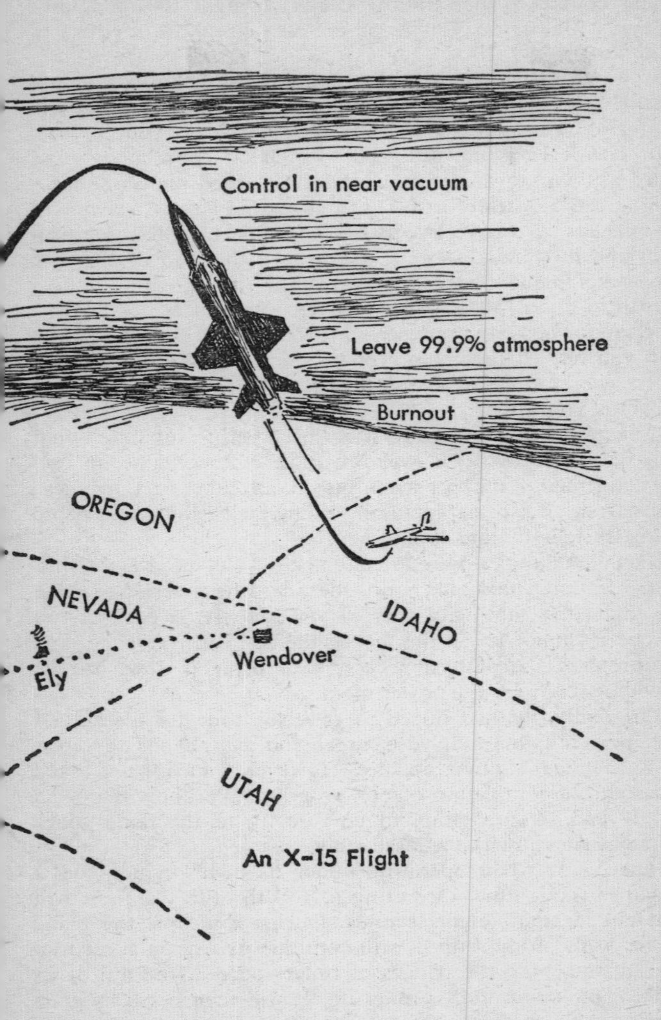

An X-15 Flight

you're going to get better acquainted with the X-15 almost immediately."

The colonel turned to the major, a man in his middle thirties. "Major, do you want to talk about the method of taking up the X-15?"

Major Coppard nodded. "I'm going to be flying with you—at least part of the way," he said, "which is to say that I'm commanding the crew on the B-52 that acts as your mother ship. The X-15 is not designed to take off from the ground under its own power. It is taken aloft attached under the right wing of a B-52 Stratofortress, just about the largest airplane in the business. We have two B-52s available here for this program and they have been altered to take the load of carrying this rocket plane under the wing until its take-off. I'll take you up to about 30,000 feet, run up to about 500 miles per hour, and when you're ready, I'll disconnect the X-15, and drop you off. At that point you're already in the air, already have a good launching speed, and can then start your engines and go on your own.

"But up to that point, you'll be just a cargo for me. You'll all get a chance to look over the B-52 mother plane, in fact as I understand the program, you'll all take part in these flights from all aspects, including riding inside the mother ship during the take-off and countdown."

The colonel took up the briefing again. "Our program is this. First, beginning this afternoon, there will be a series of glide tests under the piloting of each of you four. After each of you has had a chance to get the feel of the X-15 in free glide, and has mastered the pattern necessary to bring it down safely, we will be ready for the power flight.

"Originally, we had hoped to have the time for a series of short power flights to give each of you the chance to direct the X-15 under its own engines. However, I have been asked to hasten the completion of our program. We know the X-15 will fly and we are going to go directly to the main space flight experiment with the least delay.

"The X-15, when operating under its own engines, has a limited burnout time. Operating at full throttle the fuels will burn out in eighty-eight seconds. During this time the plane will be rising straight up. It will continue its rise on sheer momentum, reaching the fringes of outer space at the top of its climb, some one hundred miles up. It will then begin its glide down, re-entering the atmosphere. This re-entry is the most dangerous part of the flight, for here you will encounter the heat of friction. You will take it down as a glider, and when low enough land it as a glider.

"Each of you four will take the plane up once as a glider. While one of you is in the cockpit, two others will follow behind the X-15 in F-100 chase planes. Your duties will be to observe the actions of the rocket plane in the air and to advise the pilot of any dangers, or problems that you may see coming up and which he may not be aware of. The fourth astronaut will ride inside the B-52, observing the flight pattern from there and the operations of the crew serving the plane from there.

"During the rest of this morning, we will have a question-and-discussion session right here. You can and should ask anything you want to of Major Coppard, Mr. Moultrie and Mr. Lentz. If there is anything you are uncertain of, or unclear on, talk it over now and we will see if it can be cleared up."

The colonel paused, looked around. "I have one more announcement to make. It will not be possible to make more than one glide test a day, due to the time needed to prepare launching, and due to the necessity of careful checking before and after these flights. We are allowing the next week for this. The flight this afternoon will be piloted by Rod Harger. Johnny Bluehawk and Mike Mars—uh, I mean Samson here—will man the chase planes. Lannigan will ride the mother ship.

"If all goes well, one of you will take up the X-15 seven days from now on man's first visit to outer space."

Mike exhaled slowly and long. Rod sat hunched up, a thin-lipped tight grin on his face. He was going to be the first to glide it. Maybe he'd be the first also to break out beyond Earth's atmosphere. Maybe Cahoon wouldn't have to go into action after all.

CHAPTER 8

SPACE SUIT FOR ONE

THE FOUR astronauts lunched together at the cafeteria in the NASA building. They chatted lightly trying to avoid the subject of the afternoon's trial. But they were all keyed up. After all the preliminary work, after their long hours spent in the centrifuge under painful pressures and the strains of learning to fly a dummy plane, they were facing the real thing.

Mike glanced around, back at the others. "Gosh, only one week to the big flight itself. That's rushing things."

Rod Harger drank his coffee, nodded. "Glad to get it over with. The plane's been tested before. We know our abilities. It's good we don't have to go through the long business of taking short power flights, even though it would be helpful."

Mike ran a hand through his unruly brush of hair, shoved it back. "I think the colonel wanted us to have those short power flights, but time is pressing he said. Now what do you suppose he's getting pushed for?"

"We'll not know and maybe it's better we don't," said Lannigan, the lanky Navy pilot. "Remember he told us that this Space Task Group Q is a crash program. The fact is that they're taking risks with us that they'd never dare take with professional test pilots."

"I'm game," said Mike. "After all, we volunteered. This matter of outer space is a race—and I guess we're the fellows selected for the advance scouts. We're expendable, as they used to say during wartime."

"Let's not get gloomy," said Johnny Bluehawk, pushing away from the table. "They aren't going to give us any risks they don't think we can handle. Shall we get down to the hangar?"

The others followed the lead of their Cheyenne comrade and made their way to the front of the building, where a blue-painted car from the base motor pool was awaiting them. They piled in, yet as they made the trip across the hangars edging the main landing field, they were silent. The car drew up in the lot behind the base operations building and they piled out, walked across.

"Hey, look at that!" said Mike suddenly, and pointed to a strange object standing among the parked cars. The three stopped and stared at it in amusement, it seemed so out of place.

It was an old Model A Ford, standing high and primly upright amid the sleek streamlined cars on the lot around it. It was painted a light-brown and was in very good condition for a car that must have been built in the twenties, long before Mike or the others had been born.

"Now what's that doing in a place like Edwards, where everything's straining towards the future not the past?" Lannigan remarked. "It sure looks funny here."

"I can tell you," Johnny Bluehawk said. "In fact one of us may be driving that in another week."

"What!" came from the other three in unison.

The young Cheyenne nodded his head. "There's a pilots' club here at Edwards that own and run these oldtime Fords. They do it for a hobby. And it's a tradition that whoever gets to fly the most advanced plane at the base gets this car. This car has belonged to some famous pilots in its time. Whoever is finally picked to fly the X-15 will get presented with this car. So don't laugh. You may get to be the next to have to change its tires and crank its old engine."

The others chuckled and walked on towards the hangar, but Rod Harger looked back at the car and narrowed his eyes. He was wondering whether he ought to paint it a different color next week when it became his. He thought a nice bright green would look good.

Things were humming at the field when the boys arrived. The B-52 was already out of its hangar and standing on the field and there was a group of little yellow vehicles around it, fueling, checking and working in a cluster around one wing. The four walked over towards it.

The B-52 was truly a gigantic plane when seen close up. Its dimensions gave the impression of an ocean liner compared with a motor launch. It was actually only 157 feet in length but standing as it did over forty feet high, you simply felt dwarfed alongside the monster bomber. Silver in color, it seemed waiting to carry whatever huge cargo its masters wanted to load on it. Mike knew it could tote up to 450,000 pounds and it was no surprise when you saw how big it was.

"Hey, look at that!" Mike said.

Yet right now it was going to carry only a very slight load compared with its possibilities. The slight load was the 13,000 pounds of the X-15 with its fuel tanks empty. That, and the slight weight of Rod Harger, was its cargo for this afternoon.

The black X-15 looked even smaller when hanging under the mighty Stratofortress' wing. Fastened by strong metal braces under the broad wing between the body and the innermost of the double pair of jet engines on the right wing it might almost have been mistaken for some new elongated jet engine they were trying out.

As the four young fellows walked over to watch, technicians on rolling framework ladders were checking the grip of the connecting frame, and others were going through the careful final check of the X-15 itself.

Colonel Drummond detached himself from a group of men near the entry port of the mother ship. He went over to the boys. "Ready?" he asked them. They nodded.

He looked at his watch, glanced at the workmen on the plane. "They're finishing up rapidly," he said. "So let's get started." He turned and pointed to a large yellow van standing a little away from the plane.

"Rod," he said, "that's where you'll change into the MC-2 full pressure suit you'll wear. You all have tried it on and worn it in the centrifuge studies, but out here on the field, this van is fitted out to make it easy to change into your flying equipment."

"Why's that?" asked Mike. "Why not change in the regular way, in operations?"

The colonel smiled oddly. "Feel warm?" he asked.

Mike was puzzled. "Why sure," he said. "It's plenty hot, sir. It's the Mojave Desert and Southern California. But it gets cold at night."

"Sure it gets cold at night, but we're not doing this at night. At Edwards it can get very hot during mid-day, and especially as we approach the summer. Right now it's April and it's already quite hot," said the colonel. "Do you know what would happen if you put on that full pressure suit and all its protective undergarments, and tried to walk out here from the hangar or from operations?" He didn't wait for an answer, but went on. "You'd collapse of the heat inside that suit before you ever reached the plane."

"It seems they have had this problem out here in the hot desert many times. They found the way to beat it was to fit out an air-conditioned motor van to change in. When the pilot is ready and the plane is ready, all he has to do is walk a few feet from the van to the plane in his heavy suit. So we save a lot of energy and heat exhaustion."

Rod Harger started off to the big van. Mike and the others looked after him, as he came up to the huge yellow trailer-truck, which bore on its side the emblem of the Air Force Flight Test Center and a different and rather funny emblem depicting a space-suited man tied to a skyrocket. Two airmen opened the doors in the back and assisted Rod up the steps, closing the doors after him.

Mike looked after Rod a moment, then turned and watched the goings-on at the B-52. He let his clear gray eyes roam over the gigantic plane, appreciating its size and might. His eyes fell on a line of strange markings high up near the nose of the plane. He squinted at them, as he saw that they were a whole series of tiny drawings of the X-15, arranged in two long rows.

Most of the little outlines were on a level line, but here and there one was shooting diagonally upward or downward with a little jet of red shooting from it. One of the crew men, who was passing by, saw him looking at the markings, stopped and volunteered enlightenment.

"We paint a little X-15 on that space every time we do a *mission*. The ones on a level represent glide flights or just captive tryouts. The ones with a flame going up or down are the times the X-15 made power flights either upward or downward."

Mike thanked him. "Going to be some more on that line real quick," he said. Just then he saw the colonel wave at him to come over. He went to join his two friends.

"Now you three," said the colonel. "Better go to your stations. Samson and Bluehawk, report to base ops, change into your stuff, and you'll be assigned your chase planes. Lannigan, stick with me. I'll be going up in the B-52 also."

Mike and Johnny turned on their heels and went swiftly back down the line of hangars to the low pale-green building of base operations. He saw ground crew men readying two fast silvery jet planes nearby. Those would be the chase planes. He felt good. It was great to get back into action again.

CHAPTER 9

LANDING PATTERN

As MIKE and Johnny came bustling out of the operations building to get to their planes, Mike remarked in a whisper, "Now don't go taking coffee from strangers, Johnny."

The young Indian chuckled. It had become a standing gag between them although the incident referred to had been anything but a laughing matter. Mike was recalling the attempt made at Wright Field a few months ago to drug Johnny when he was piloting their first zero gravity test flight. If it hadn't been for Mike's quick action and the fact that Mike himself never drank coffee, they would both have been killed. Ever since then this little remark was passed between them every time they donned their flying equipment.

Actually, Mike thought to himself, as they neared the two Super Sabres, it might be that they were closer to the mysterious saboteur who had tried to destroy them at that time than they had been in a while. That curious sneak exploration of the X-15 hangar had the mark of something. He shook his head to expel the thought and reached the plane waiting for him.

It was a standard F-100 such as he had flown many times in the past. It was one of several used regularly at the Air Force Flight Test Center for observation purposes and as he came up to it his eye rested for a moment on the bright orange painted tail on which was painted the insignia of the base.

It was symbolic, Mike thought, of what they were doing. It was a shield divided in half diagonally. The lower half showed the gray-brown of desert with two cacti on it. The top half the black of space with a golden rocket streaming blue flames heading upward. Beneath the shield was the inscription, *Ad Inexplorata*—To the Unexplored.

He climbed into the tight cockpit, fitted in his earphones, and began the regular checking of the ship that all Air Force pilots make before taking off. When this was accomplished without a hitch, he reported himself ready to the control tower.

Looking out across the field he could see the little yellow

vehicles moving away from the B-52, whose mighty jets had already begun their roar of preparation. He could make out the X-15 slung under its wing and since the van had moved away, he guessed that Rod was already in its tiny airtight cabin, ready to go. He slid the canopy shut, and over the earphones he caught Major Coppard's voice.

"Harger?" said the B-52's commander. There was a word of acknowledgment. "Bluehawk?" Another voice came in, Johnny's. "Samson?" Mike answered. It was a hookup among all parties.

The major told them what he planned. Mike and Johnny taxied out to the runway, readied for take-off. As they jockied into line, Mike could hear the B-52 beginning its slow run into position. There were the sounds of the mother ship's cockpit check, followed by Harger's voice okaying the readings in the rocket ship's cockpit still snugly attached to the big plane's right wing.

The order came at last. Mike shot off down the runway and took off, followed closely by Johnny. They rose high, and circled the field, watching what went on below.

The B-52 now rumbled down the long runway and became airborne, rising steadily and powerfully higher and higher. At command, Mike and Johnny wheeled about and followed it as the huge bomber rose up into the thinner air and raced on, north and east of the field.

Mike kept his plane as close to the B-52 as he dared for it was his duty to try never to let its little black spaceship companion out of his sight. The major kept them advised at all times of his plans. Now, after several minutes, they had reached the height wanted, for Mike's altimeter registered 38,000 feet and the air was thin and the ground far down diminished to the proportions of a miniature map of desert and stumpy hills.

The B-52 came around in a wide circle. "Ready to drop," came the major's voice.

"Ready, sir," came Harger's voice back.

"One minute warning," said the B-52.

Harger spoke again. "Everything O.K."

"Chase planes, prepare to follow drop."

"Ready, sir," said Mike and Johnny in unison as their Super Sabres completed the same swing around and ran along with the B-52 at identical speed.

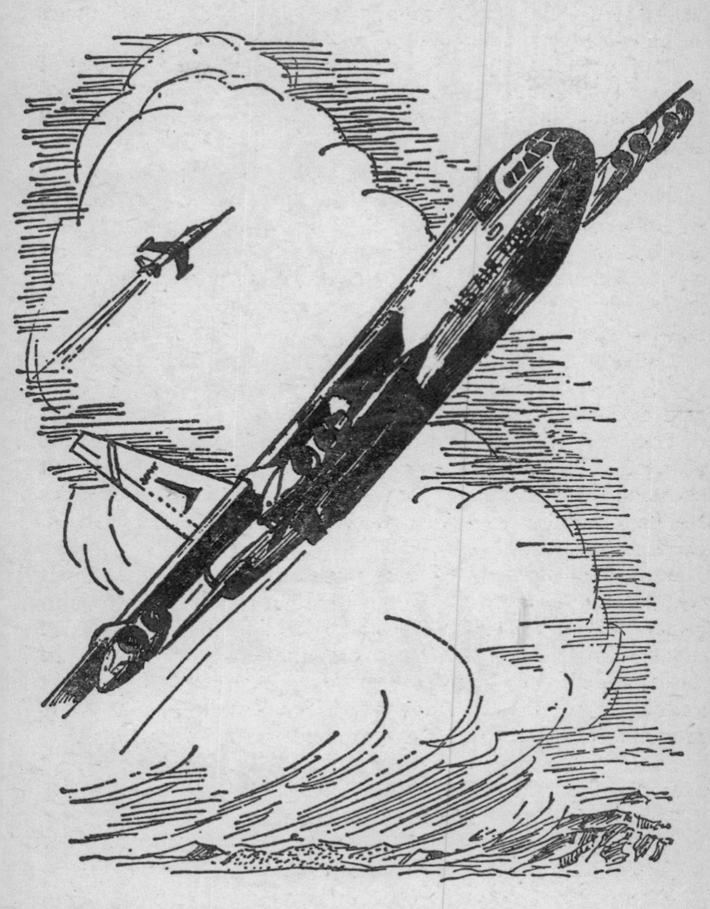

The B-52 rose into the air higher and higher.

The black dart shot out and down.

"Countdown for drop beginning," said the B-52. There was a pause. Then, "Five. Four. Three. Two. One——

"Drop!"

Someone pushed a switch. The grapples holding the X-15 to the wing clicked open.

Mike saw the black dartlike shape suddenly fall away from the Stratofortress' wing. It shot out and down, for the moment strikingly like a black paper dart flung by the hand of a boy.

Its speed, Mike knew from his own gauges, was 500 miles per hour. As it dropped, Mike knew Harger would have to keep it level and gliding steadily.

Mike swung his plane and began to follow it down. He spoke into his throat mike:

"You're doing nicely, Rod. Still leveling, and well away from the B-52."

Johnny's voice came in, checking his.

The black plane swung out turning toward the distant marking of Edwards like a tiny toy structure far below. It soared easily now, yet seemed to be approaching the ground at a still rapid rate. Mike spoke up, described this to Rod, who acknowledged briefly.

"Wind check, please," said Harger now. Mike responded, gave him the direction of the wind. There was a set landing pattern to be used by the X-15 and Rod was following instructions carefully.

Edwards was visible more plainly now. They had lost altitude, down to 20,000 feet already. Swiftly the X-15, a black dart before Mike's eyes, turned its bullet nose and described a flat arc. Rod was bringing it upwind, so that the flow of air could brake it. Now they were nearly over Edwards, at 18,000 feet.

The X-15 slid down, against the wind, taking full advantage of the current. Mike and Johnny followed right on its tail, checking their indicators all the way and keeping Rod advised as to how far he had gone and what their readings were.

"Six thousand, five hundred feet," called Mike.

At this point, with Edwards and its runways already clearly lined up beneath them, the X-15 swung around, and began to lower still further, this time flying with the air currents rather than against them.

This was the ticklish point, Mike realized and felt himself a little damp from anxiety. In his mind, as they went, he was riding with Harger, and he knew instinctively, from his many hours of patient training, exactly what Rod would be thinking and doing.

The lower to the ground the more risky the little spaceship was. It was a heavy ship for its size, for it was an all-metal ship, braced against the heat and friction of its space-flying purpose. It was a difficult ship to glide for its narrow wing surfaces would not suffice should its speed fall too much, yet its minimum speed in flight was far greater than a normal plane should have for landing.

The X-15 glided on, with the wind. Below it Edwards moved away, and the large flat yellow-gray surface of Rogers Dry Lake appeared. This was the place that Harger would bring the black ship down.

Rogers Dry Lake and others like it in the vicinity was a principal reason why the Air Force Flight Test Center had been built out there in the Mojave Desert. The dry lake was a flat expanse of what had once been lake bed a thousand years ago. Now no water flowed there. But where waves had once flowed back and forth there was now a dry lake bottom, as flat as a table top and as hard-packed as a concrete pavement.

This remarkable natural table made a perfect landing field for planes, and because of the many experimental planes flying out of Edwards at all times, landings on these dry lakes were as safe as runway landings. Any pilot in trouble—and test pilots might find themselves in trouble at any time—could feel safe in making one of these lake bottoms his emergency field.

"Three thousand, six hundred feet," said Mike and Johnny at the same time. And even as they said it, they saw the X-15 turn about once more, head into the wind and begin to come down.

Mike found himself holding his breath. This was the moment of danger, the point at which even expert test pilots had had trouble.

The X-15 was still holding a speed of 250 miles an hour and the flat surface of Rogers Dry Lake was now a few hundred feet away. As it sped along, the nose of the X-15 lifted slightly and the tail began to sag.

Had this happened with any other plane, Mike would have called out in alarm, but this was the right way for the rocket ship. For instead of conventional landing wheels, it had skids at the rear which would take up the initial shock of landing. With other planes the bulk of the weight would be in the front or in the wings, making a landing on the front wheels practical, but the heavy rocket engine in the back of the plane made it tail-heavy.

Down Rod came, the two chase planes swooping along at his heels.

There was a split-second when the black ship seemed to hang just above the ground. Then the skid struck and as it raced along the bed of the lake bottom a cloud of dust arose like a cloud of smoke.

The black ship seemed to hang on that skid for seconds and then the nose swung down, the front wheels, just under the nose, hit the ground, sent up a second spume of dust, and then, all safely on the ground, the X-15 raced across the lake bed slowing down and finally after a long track had been scratched across the hard surface, came to a stop.

Mike and Johnny swooped low over it, but they saw nothing amiss. No sign of fire, no damage, Then they, too, swung around, came down low on the dry lake bed, and brought their two ships down near the quiet metal body of the X-15.

As the two astronauts threw back the canopies of their F-100s, they could see the lines of dust following the yellow dots that were engineers and ambulance men and ground crew racing out to meet them.

A *good job, Rod,* thought Mike. *Can I do as well tomorrow?*

CHAPTER 10

SPACEMAN'S INITIALS

THERE was a knock on Rod Harger's door. Rod had already retired, turned his light out, gone to bed tired and elated from the flight that afternoon. Outside it was dark and the other three astronauts had also hit the sack in their separate rooms down the long hall.

Rod sat up in bed, reached over and switched on the desk light. Again came the knocking, soft, but insistent. The stocky young man with the pale straw hair and the cold eyes slipped out of bed, padded over to the door, opened it a crack.

The man outside pushed out a hand, shoved the door open and hastily slipped inside, closing it behind him. Rod stared at him. "Oh, it's you," he said finally.

"Yeah," said the gaunt man with the small hooked scar on his face, "it's me. Don't look so surprised. Your old man must have told you I was around."

Rod locked the door and sat down on his bed. "No, he never mentioned it," he said in a low voice. "But I had a suspicion that prowler who broke into the X-15 building was you."

The man who called himself Cahoon nodded. "You guessed right. I admit it. It was a boneheaded thing to do, but I thought I might spot something practical."

Rod nodded. "It certainly was useless. You might have gotten caught. Besides, I think I have this thing well in hand without your help. My father only wanted to make sure I was one of the seven astronauts. I can do the rest myself."

Cahoon frowned, shook his head. "I ain't taking any chances. There's too much in it now for me to quit—and your father agrees with me. I'm sticking close to you all the way until you're the first on the Moon. Besides, this is personal with me. I'm going to get that Mike Mars if its the last thing I do. So you better work with me."

Rod felt himself getting hot. "I don't want your help. I can make my own way here. This X-15—there's nothing you can do to it that wouldn't be plain downright sabotage. You'd be

"Don't pull that stuff on me," Cahoon said.

helping the enemies of our country more than you'd be helping me, and whether you like it or not, I don't want to be a traitor."

The man called Cahoon snarled. "Nuts, kid. You're in too deep to pull that patriotic stuff on me. Besides, I know all about the Air Force—I was in it until they threw me out. I've got it in for them too. If one X-15 is blown up or crashes, they got two others and they can make more."

Rod sat there, furious but silent. Cahoon's threat was all too clear. He was in too deep. He couldn't tell on the saboteur, he couldn't stop him without destroying his own career. He wanted to be the first man on the Moon, he wanted that fame and glory that his father had held before him, and the money that he could make from it also.

But deep down he had a pride in himself and the Air Force. He wanted to do it on his own. After all, hadn't he been picked to be the first to glide the X-15? Didn't that mean that they thought highly of him, that he had a good chance of being the first to crack outer space in it next week? Why did he need to get mixed up now with trickery and crime and . . . maybe murder.

Cahoon sensed the boy's conflicting thoughts. He leaned forward, tapped his chest with a hard finger. "Let's get this straight. You're going to help me as much as I need and that's that. I'm going out to get Mike Mars and anyone else that nudges you out. So . . . I came here to get the schedule. What's the plans for the big flight up?"

Harger sat back. He realized he was defeated. Once mixed up in this, there was no way he could clear himself and save his chances. He got up, went to the desk, picked up some notes he'd been given. Bringing them over to his night visitor, he explained what was to happen the next week and the following.

Cahoon asked a few questions, then nodded slowly. "The time that's important is next Monday. That's when the big flight is taking place. Now I understand you to say that the mother plane first flies out with the X-15 already fueled to Wendover, Utah, then starts back. The X-15 is dropped as they near Ely, Nevada, and then starts its power flight upward. O.K. I figured as much and I've got my plans already made. I've lined up a couple of hard-boiled eggs to help me. As soon as you know that you aren't the one that's going to fly that Monday, just blink your light in this room three times at exactly eleven o'clock at night. I'll be watching each night. When I see that, I'll go into action. And God help you if you try to hold back on me."

"What are you going to do?" asked Rod.

Cahoon shook his head. "You'll find out when I'm ready," he said, getting up and going to the door. "I'll be seeing you, pal." He slipped out as quietly as he had come in.

Rod Harger sat down on his bed and put his head in his hands. He was shaking, but he saw no way out of it. At last he put out the light, went to bed.

The next day it was Mike's turn to take the X-15 down in a glider action. They spent the morning observing at the B-52 and the maintenance building. The model of the X-15 used yesterday was still undergoing a careful check, and it would be one of the other two that would be taken up in this day's flight.

The morning passed faster than Mike knew, and it seemed to Mike that time had truly taken wings when he found himself walking up the steps into the big yellow van next to the B-52 on the field. It was already afternoon, the scene was the same as yesterday's, but now he was going into the trailer-truck, and Rod Harger and Jack Lannigan would be flying the chase planes. Johnny had slapped him on the back just a few seconds ago, and had gone to take his place in the B-52's launching hold.

Inside the van, two technicians helped him remove his uniform and climb into the MC-2 suit. He had worn it before or one that resembled it, but as he drew on the slip-knit nylon suit, which fit bulkily but comfortably over him, and as the helpers were testing it for airtight seams, it dawned on him that he was taking another step in his dream of getting to Mars.

For the MC-2 suit was actually the first fully workable space suit. In that outfit Mike could have stepped out on the surface of the Moon and lived. It was the suit to be worn in a spaceship, and the X-15 was a spaceship.

Unlike other pressure suits worn by aviators at high levels, this suit created and maintained its own artificial atmosphere, yet it was light of weight and not as constricting and rigid as the G-suits Mike had worn. Over the basic suit, the men fitted an aluminum-colored outer coverall, which held his parachute-restrain harness and, in a back-pack, contained his pressure controls for the suit.

A frame like that of a deep-sea diver was the neck of the all-enclosing outfit, and over Mike's head the two helpers lifted the white helmet with the unbreakable face plate and screwed it tight. When Mike pulled down the face mask, it would snap into place and complete the closed inner atmosphere of the suit, which made the wearer entirely independent of outside airlessness or extremes of cold or heat.

Mike held up a hand. "Any of you fellows got a crayon or a thick pencil?"

"I got one," said one of the helpers and dug a thick black marking crayon out of a box on a shelf. "What do you want it for?"

"Take it and write my initials on the front of the helmet," Make said. "That's my good luck mark."

"What's the initials, Lieutenant Samson?" asked the airman with the cryon.

"M.A.R.S." said Mike. "That's me."

The helper carefully printed the four letters on his helmet. "Hey," he said, "that spells Mars. You going there?"

"Someday, mister, someday," said Mike, getting up and walking to the closed doors of the van. "You think they're ready out there?"

"Ready when you are, sir," said the helpers, and pushing the doors open, helped Mike down the stairs and across the few feet of hot Mojave air to the ladder leading to the cockpit of the X-15.

CHAPTER 11

CHARIOT FOR A HIGH-FLIER

FROM the moment that Mike Mars seated himself in the form-fitting seat inside the tiny cabin cockpit of the X-15 he felt secure and confident. He had studied the setup so carefully, he had dreamed so long for so many years of his young life of sitting someday at the controls of a spaceship, that now it seemed but natural that he should do so.

Yet he could not deny that he felt thrills run up and down his spine. It was, somehow, as if a dream had actually begun to take solid shape and form. For there was no question that this black plane was a spaceship in every sense of the word.

It was reinforced against external heat and cold. It had its own internal atmosphere, able to be kept up against whatever might be outside. It was cool and comfortable, although the desert air outside was hot and not at all pleasant for one as heavily dressed as he in the space suit he wore. With the canopy down, with only the slanting narrow windows to give him a limited view of the field in front, he was already enclosed in a man-made world separate from Mother Earth. It now required only to be carried aloft, there to soar upward on wings of flame.

Not this time however. The fuel gauges on his dashboard showed the giant tanks that composed most of his ship to be empty.

He plugged in the various connections of his suit to their connections knowing that on doing so he was connecting his own bodily reactions to the scrutiny of observers. He answered the voice that came over his earphones, reported himself ready.

The take-off of the B-52, the conversations with chase planes and the mother ship, the instructions, the checkout, the final drop countdown, all went along with an easy speed that proved his hours of concentration had not been in vain. In every respect they followed the experience of yesterday, but now Rod Harger's voice was in the plane that had held Johnny Bluehawk and Jack Lannigan's came from the jet that had been Mike's.

As the X-15 suddenly dropped free, Mike grasped the con-

trols firmly, and his mind took over coolly and automatically the task of gliding the spaceship down to the ground five miles below.

At that instant, he felt himself utterly calm, with a sort of detached coolness taking over his body. Now he was part of the machine and he moved precisely and swiftly to guide the ship down.

This strange detachment was no surprise to him. This was a product of self-training from the time of his boyhood, from the day when he first swore to himself that he would make his destination Mars and would not be turned from his goal.

He had at that time made himself three rules of conduct as the means to attain that ambition, and these rules had led him straight and true to the achievement of all that he had set after.

The first had been to maintain his good health, by avoiding laziness, overindulgence, by respect for his body and his muscles, and by refusing to allow his system to be poisoned by heavy smoking or drinking.

The second had been to keep his brain firmly disciplined to study and understanding. Proficiency in his lessons, the ability to learn new things fast and accurately—these were the keys to mastery of the world around him.

The third was to keep his faith, never to allow doubt to cause him to waver from his ambition or to lose confidence in his own ability to rise above any temporary setbacks.

He had made these principles the rule of his life and they had never played him false. Now, at the moment of trial, he drew on them for power—and found them responding fully.

He brought the X-15 down to a safe landing on Rogers Dry Lake in exactly the proper fashion. His turns, his reports, his split-second reactions to wind and altitude and stability were almost mechanical in their perfection. The good performance of Rod Harger the day before was matched in every way by Mike's handling of the spaceship.

Once the X-15 had come to a complete halt, Mike waited inside the closed cabin. To attempt to leave would be unwise, for the suit he wore required the presence of the van nearby to avoid the risk of heat prostration. But outside he saw the two chase planes roll to a landing, and waved from inside as the two pilots got out and walked over to him, just before the caravan of cars arrived from the main field.

In the next two days, the story was repeated. First Johnny Bluehawk glided the X-15 down, without a hitch, and then

He brought the X-15 to a safe landing.

Jack Lannigan repeated the story. To Mike's eyes, all four glides seemed quite perfect. But the real story as to which of the four would make the best risk for the power flight to outer space would not depend on the way the flights had looked.

From that viewpoint they all were quite well handled. The real decision would come from the records gathered by the telemetering equipment at the NASA building roof. There, on tapes and charts, were recorded the secrets that none of the pilots or observers could suspect. The actual heartbeats of the pilots— were the heartbeats of one pilot faster than another? The bodily heat—did one of the pilots betray inner uncertainty, raise a faint temperature, breathe harder under strain? The rate of burning oxygen in the lungs—was there a tattletale of nervous energy from these readings.

The instruments would not lie, and they would show unmistakably which of the four was the coolest under strain, which the most level-headed, which the least exhausted. They also would show whether any strains had been registered on the X-15 by the pilot's handling, subtle though they may be.

By these things a decision would be reached as to the best man to take up the X-15 in its master flight, for however slight the difference between one of the keen young men and another, nothing must be omitted to make the trip a success.

The four astronauts were understandably on edge during the Friday of that week. That was the day the decision would come down as to who was to be the first to take up the X-15 on Monday. There was now already some question as to whether the others would be able to take it up in following trips. The colonel had indicated that time was pressing for the next phase of Project Quicksilver—there were three other astronauts whose training elsewhere for that next phase was evidently approaching some decision.

Possibly there might be time now for only the one flight—the big attempt to reach outer space. Which would be the fortunate pilot?

They spent their time that Friday studying movies and photos of the X-15 in power flight. With them was Kent Scott and the others who had been present at those flights and each of the four tried to store away as many hints as he could from the experiences that had gone before. Each saw himself at the controls, rocketing along under mighty power.

While they studied, Colonel Drummond, Dr. Holderlin, Frank Moultrie, and other scientists were huddled in conference, checking the records of the four flights, checking the records of the four men's past experiences and abilities at the dummy controls.

It was growing late in the afternoon when the four astronauts finished their studies. Nobody had yet told them the decision. They started out of the NASA building, on their way back to quarters to wash up and have their dinner. As they emerged they looked around for the Air Force car they had phoned for.

The blue car, driven by its airman chauffeur, was waiting for them. Standing beside it was Kent Scott. As the four young men walked up to the car, Kent smiled.

"Hi, fellows. There isn't room for all of you in this car, so one of you will have to go separately.

"Mike, can you drive?"

Mike Mars nodded. "Sure can. Am I the one that gets left out?"

Kent waved a hand. "Yep, you're left out. We got another car for you, though. Can you drive this one? It's a little old, but it's yours now."

Mike followed his hand's direction. Parked to one side at the entrance of the building was a funny-looking light-brown car, a Model A Ford. With a sudden start he recognized the car. He felt his ears burning, and something like an electric spark shot through his spine.

"I—I—ugh—guess I can drive it," he managed to get out.

"Well, come on then," said Kent. "I'll ride with you and show you how to keep the old bucket of bolts from falling apart."

The three others suddenly caught on. They remembered Johnny Bluehawk's words, "Whoever gets to fly the most advanced plane at the base gets this car."

And Mike had got it.

At eleven o'clock that night, after all four of the astronauts had put out their room lights and gone to bed, a light flashed on in one of their rooms. It blinked on and off three times, then went out again.

CHAPTER 12

ACTION STATIONS

JOHNNY BLUEHAWK awoke with a start. The room was dark and he lay there in bed wondering what had startled him. He heard a door open somewhere down the hall and quiet footsteps move. Some latecomer, he thought, probably that was what woke him out of his sleep.

It was still early, not quite midnight. He turned over in bed to go back to sleep. Faintly he heard muffled voices from somewhere down the hall. He wondered sleepily where and decided the noise might be coming from the next room, perhaps some late conversation between two of the other people staying on their floor.

Then he remembered that the next room down the hall from his was Rod Harger's. So that couldn't be where the voices were coming from, because Rod must be as asleep as they were. Besides—who would have business with Rod at that hour? Dismissing the sound from his mind, Johnny closed his eyes again, drifted back to sleep.

The next room was dark, but Rod was sitting up in bed. Someone had come in the door, which had been left unlocked, and that someone was perched on the edge of Rod's bed. There were questions asked in a hushed voice, and Rod answered as best he could.

Then, "I'll need the key to one of the storehouses. It'll be on the rack in base operations. Get it for me, tomorrow."

"How can I do that?" whispered Rod. "They don't just hand out things like that."

"Never mind how," said Cahoon. "Borrow it when nobody's looking. You can do it. Hang around there until you get the chance. But I must have it. The storehouse is in building——"

He whispered the number and location. Rod argued back beneath his breath, but Cahoon was insistent. Finally he got up, started tiptoeing to the door. "I'll be in the cafeteria building near the field at one o'clock. See that you meet me there with the key. Don't let anybody spot you."

Rod was still protesting, but the soft click of the closing door

Borrow the key, Cahoon had said.

told him his visitor had left. He lay back in bed, angry and a little scared. He'd told Cahoon of the schedule, now he was only getting himself in deeper.

The next day was no weekend holiday. To get the X-15's power flight ready for Monday was exceedingly short notice, but Drummond seemed anxious to cut out further delay. Everybody connected with the project was alerted and in action. The model to be used was being checked very carefully and readied. The B-52 was undergoing a careful check out.

At the NASA headquarters, the four astronauts met in the morning for a quick run-down on the coming event. They gathered before a map of the vast area the Air Force had set aside as its high range flight area. This covered a space of hundreds of miles ranging from the Mojave in Southern California clear up to the Bonneville Salt Flats in the corner of Utah, stretching out across the state of Nevada between.

Colonel Drummond pointed out the various features that concerned them on the map.

"The X-15 will be taken by air as far as Wendover Air Base in Utah. At that point, the B-52 will turn around, start flying back. The X-15 will be dropped as we near Ely, Nevada, and will start its power climb at once. As it proceeds, the B-52 will follow along the same track, and the chase planes as well. We estimate the X-15 will descend back into the atmosphere and come into sight of the mother plane and chase planes somewhere between Ely and Beatty, in Nevada. It will then glide on to the region of Edwards and make its descent to the ground.

"Now there are three stations from which the X-15 will be checked continuously by telemetry and radar. One of these is at Ely, the second at Beatty, the third right here. None of the three stations will ever be out of contact with the plane and its pilot at any time. The NASA staff are already moving out to the two stations at Beatty and Ely and getting them ready for operations. Frank Moultrie will head the staff out at Ely, which is the first station to contact the spaceship and which will get the best coverage of its rocket flight period."

The four astronauts studied the flight track with concentration. "What will be the roles assigned to the rest of us?" asked Jack Lannigan.

"The chase planes to be used in this operation will be manned by Bluehawk and Harger. You will be based in the mother ship."

"Will the rest of us get a chance to fly the X-15 after this first flight?" asked Harger in a soft tone.

"If time permits, and everything goes all right, we may be able to get another flight perhaps by Thursday. If we have the chance, I will say that we have picked you, Harger, for it."

Rod tightened his lips. *And if something does not go right,* he thought to himself, *you will need to make a second attempt, just to save face and save the project. Cahoon knows what he's doing, after all.*

The four broke up, as Kent Scott came in, gathered up Mike Mars and took him down the hall to go over previous power trials of the X-15. Mike would spend the rest of the day studying the records, second-by-second, of the X-15's powered flights while Kent Scott would dredge up every memory he had of the problems that had come up during them. They would attempt to cover in advance every possible trick and mishap the X-15 might do.

As Kent explained, "Most of the bugs have been ironed out on this final model. We think we've got the rocket ship licked. But you've got to be prepared for everything."

While Mike was concentrating on this, Lannigan went around to work with the B-52 crew on their preparation.

Johnny and Rod went out to the field, first to study their chase planes again—although there was little to be done on them. They were thoroughly familiar with these speedy jet fighters and the ground crews would see that they were in perfect condition.

They went to the base operations to go over the maps of the course. This gave Rod the opportunity he was looking for. He prowled around the offices until he located the keys he sought. Finding the opportunity to slip the keys off their hook was not easy, but with a little intentional interruption of the man on duty, he managed the trick, although he was damp with perspiration from the nervous strain.

He found a pretense of excusing himself from Johnny Bluehawk, slipped out, and made his way to the cafeteria.

Johnny Bluehawk was aware that Rod was bothered, but he put it down to the stocky astronaut's rivalry with Mike. Johnny knew that although Rod had been on Mike's team back in training days, as had Johnny himself, he'd never been really friendly. Johnny had often wondered just how much Rod had been involved in the events that had caused so much trouble for Mike and himself during the days of their tests.

The young Cheyenne, who had overcome a great deal of hardship and often prejudice to qualify for the Air Force and to win his wings, knew that on several occasions Rod had supposedly made ugly remarks about Mike and his "Redskin" pal. Johnny had learned to keep his emotions under control, to adopt the expressionless face in the teeth of opposition, that characterized his fighting ancestors. He had refused to allow his temper to burst into flame, judging rightly that the first to lose his head would always be the real loser in any fight.

But Johnny and Mike, in talking it over, had not been able to accept that Rod, as a fellow pilot, would stoop to the outright villainy that had happened in the past.

Now Johnny, still in base operations, began to feel hungry. Glancing at his watch, he saw that it was past one. He looked around for Rod Harger, figuring that they ought to go out and get a bite of lunch.

But when he asked around, nobody seemed to know where Harger had gone. Finally, stepping outside, he found an airman who said he had seen the other astronaut going off in the direction of the cafeteria.

Johnny scratched his head. Well, maybe Harger had been

unable to find him, he told himself. So he'd go to the cafeteria and join him.

Johnny hailed a car going off in the right direction and a few minutes later was dropped off at his destination. He went into the building, looked around the eating hall.

As he glanced around, someone stood up at a table in a far corner and started toward the door, coming toward Johnny.

There was something familiar about him.

The Cheyenne's dark eyes fastened on him. There was something familiar about that man.

The stranger was in civilian clothes, obviously an engineer or a workman on the base. But his face . . . something about it reminded the Indian youth of someone else, someplace. . . .

The man brushed past Johnny as if he didn't see him, keeping his face averted. Johnny glanced after him, then turned back, searching the hall. He saw Rod's pale straw-colored hair at a table in a distant corner. Johnny started over to him, to join him for lunch. As he made his way over, he pondered the identity of the strange man.

Suddenly he stopped stock-still, almost knocking over a sergeant with a tray. Murmuring apologies, the coppery-skinned tall young man turned abruptly about, hastily made his way back to the door. He reached the door, looked out. But the stranger was gone.

Johnny Bluehawk turned back, picked up a tray, and went to get lunch. First he'd feed himself, ready himself for the hunt. Because his work for that afternoon was cut out.

He remembered that face now. It was the man who had brought him the drugged coffee back at Wright Field. It was the face of the mysterious saboteur.

If he was on this base, he could be found. Johnny didn't want to alarm Mike or disturb the careful plans for the flight. He'd track this man himself, and pin him down. His ancestors had stalked the buffalo, his grandfather had outwitted the entire United States Cavalry, and Johnny would show this paleface renegade that the blue hawk still had sharp claws.

CHAPTER 13

THE TRACKER

JOHNNY BLUEHAWK put his tray down at the same table Rod was seated at. He said nothing to the other astronaut about the mysterious stranger, for he had never entirely trusted Rod and besides he felt that it was a personal thing between himself and the man with the tiny scar on his cheek.

So he kept quiet and simply allowed an idle sort of chitchat to go on between them. Rod finished earlier, having started before him, and took his leave. Johnny finished his lunch in silence, thinking out his plans of action.

How did one go about finding a stranger, when you didn't know his name, his place of residence, his business, or what he was up to?

Johnny turned over the problem in his mind, carefully sorted it out, and finally determined that he did have several clues to work on. They were perhaps guesses, but apparently sound enough.

First, in some way the stranger was connected with the plans for the astronauts.

Again, he must be the one who had tried to probe the X-15. This meant that he was planning some sort of interference of the coming flight, the big one. Therefore, in some way his future movements must be connected with plans for that flight.

To do this, he had to be located somewhere on the base. The base was large, but located as it was out in the Mojave Desert, it was self-contained. The nearest town was many miles away and the stranger could not operate from there. There were only so many places a civilian could sleep and eat around an Air Force base such as this, though Edwards did have an unusually high number of civilians working at the various aircraft plants and the missile-testing stands in the nearby mountains.

A systematic check up at these places should turn up some track.

Johnny got up, went out. He wasted no time, for he felt that whatever this man was up to, it would have to be ready the same target day as Mike's X-15 flight. And that was now but a day and a half away.

He spent the afternoon following his thoughts. Returning to base operations, he asked around whether anyone had seen a man answering that stranger's description. But none had. He borrowed a car from the motor pool, and began to make the rounds of the base.

At the X-15 maintenance plant, he talked to O'Shaugnessy and his fellow security men. They ran over their memories of the men who worked at the plant and of recent visitors but none seemed to answer the proper description.

At NASA, nobody was able to recall anyone like that. At other plants, the security guards were no more helpful. At the Air Force headquarters there were no security guards at the doorways, but asking around produced no one who remembered anyone like the gaunt man of mystery.

At the big hangar, he wandered around asking various of the men working there, but again none had remembered such a person. Johnny was aware that all these people had their minds on more important things, but there was always the possibility of finding someone.

So the afternoon wore on, and as it began to grow late, Johnny realized he had produced no clue. Glumly he drove back to his quarters, the quadrangle of buildings that housed the bachelor officers' quarters and also served as a hotel for visitors both in uniform and out. As he came up to them, he noticed the building that housed the civilians' club, which was a restaurant off to one side of the quadrangle. As a rule, he and the other astronauts took their meals at the big officers' club set up on a hill at the far side of the quarters.

Johnny drove up and parked before this other eating place. Getting out, he went in. It was still early and there was no activity in the dining hall. He went to the cashier's desk and when that man came out of his little office, Johnny asked him the same question he had been asking all afternoon. He described the stranger, asked if he'd seen anyone answering that description.

The cashier leaned against the desk, scratched his head. "Well, I see a lot of strangers all the time around here, but I think I may have seen someone like that. Thin-faced fellow with a sort of little hooked scar?"

Johnny nodded, his face impassive but his heart suddenly jumping. The cashier thought a while longer. "Yep, I'm pretty sure I've seen him. I seem to remember him having had breakfast here several times the past couple weeks, and sometimes dinner. Eats alone, he does, and doesn't pay attention to other people."

He paused. "I think he must be staying at the BOQ because I'm pretty sure he walked here. Didn't drive up like some. He'd have to be staying there to just be able to walk in. Why don't you try around there?"

Johnny nodded, thanked him. Leaving, he drove around to the billeting office at the quarters, parked and went in. His own room was upstairs in that same building, and the three other astronauts' as well. The trail was getting close to home, he thought.

He stopped at the office, asked about the stranger. The airman who was on duty seemed puzzled for a moment, turned and asked a girl at the desk. She came over, listened to the description. "That sounds like one of the men upstairs," she said finally. "I'm pretty sure I've seen him come and go."

She drew over the registration book, went over it slowly. "Now I'm not sure of the name, but I think that he might be Mr. Cahoon." She turned the book around, pointed to the scrawled room number. "Try there."

Johnny thanked her, turned and went upstairs. The room number in question was down the hall, a good way down, but still—on the same floor.

He tried the doors of the other astronauts but none of them was back yet. The afternoon was late but they had not knocked off their work.

Johnny went quietly along to the door of Cahoon's room. It was locked, Cahoon was still away.

Coming back up the hall, he heard feet trotting up the stairs and a moment later Mike popped into view. They hailed each other. "You're off early," called Mike. "How about dinner?"

Johnny nodded. Ten minutes later the two friends walked across the sands up to the officers' club, now coming to life for the evening. The sun was low on the horizon, the sky was clear and turning faintly reddish, in the distance the line of far mountains were grayish-purple ridges against the darkening blue.

They ate leisurely and chatted about the flight to come.

Mike outlined to Johnny some of the tips he had picked up, and told him about the early troubles Kent Scott had with the X-15.

Johnny said nothing about the stranger. He realized that Mike had to have a clear and uninterrupted mind for the job facing him the day after tomorrow. This was going to be Johnny's private job.

They returned to quarters in twilight as the first faint chill of the night was creeping over the desert. From midday to midnight the temperature at this high desert shifted as much as forty or fifty degrees. "Real Martian-type weather," Mike had commented when they had first become aware of that.

He had explained then that on Mars the conditions of a high desert also prevailed, although of course far more extreme than in the Mojave. There too the temperature shift could range over fifty or more degrees in one day. On that planet also the surface must bear considerable resemblance to this same arid sandy dry desert waste.

Back on their floor, the two separated again, to resume their studies and get their early sleep. Johnny went to his room, waited a while, then slipped out. He went down to the office intending to ask whether anyone had seen Cahoon return. As he came up to the desk, the girl who had helped him before spotted him.

"Oh, sir," she said, "you just missed the man you were looking for. Mr. Cahoon just checked out."

Johnny was startled. Checked out? He kept his surprise out of his voice as he asked, "Can you lend me the key he turned in? I loaned him a book a couple nights ago and it must still be in his room."

A white lie, but the girl believed it. She gave him the key. He ran lightly up the stairs, went to the room Cahoon had just vacated, opened it and went in.

The room was quite empty. The stranger had indeed cleared out, taking whatever property he had with him. But the cleaning girl had not yet gone over the place. Johnny carefully looked around.

He opened the desk, searched the drawers. There was nothing. He looked into the waste basket. There were some scraps of paper. He dumped them out, looked through them. Nothing of value, he thought, and then his hand leaped out, picked up a tiny paper tag.

There was a number on the tag and a broken cord as if it had been attached to something. Johnny turned it over and over, thinking. Could it have been attached to a key? The number was in four digits. What could that mean?

He searched his mind. It struck him then that all the buildings on the base were numbered—and in four digits. Could this be a key to a building? And if so, which building had that number?

He returned to his room, buckled on his service revolver, slipped into a light jacket, left. At the office, he returned the key and asked if they could tell him where the building of that number was.

At first they were unfamiliar with it. But the airman found a guide and thumbing through it, found it. "It's way out at the far edge of the base, sir," he said. "It's one of the buildings used for storing special explosives and the more dangerous fuels." He took a map and pointed out to him how these storehouses were so placed as to be remote from the rest of the area in the event of accident.

Johnny thanked him, left. He went to his car, got in, and set out for the area.

It was now dark, and overhead the stars were out in great numbers. The moon was not yet up but still the stars shed a faint glow over the landscape. He drove out, past the hangars and work quarters now dark save for their security lights, out beyond the areas he was familiar with and across near the mountains.

He came to the road he sought and noted by his headlights the warning sign. He drove slowly now, then turned his lights out and parked by the side.

Johnny Bluehawk got out of the car, and walked softly forward along the dark and deserted road. His keen Indian eyes, accustomed from childhood to the night and the ways of the dark, picked out the black forms of the desert growths around him and against the star-strewn sky the black outlines of the storehouses.

He came to where the map indicated the building he sought was standing. It was off the road on a little side road all its own. He walked on soundless feet down the road.

Far off in the distance he could hear the barking of coyotes. Somewhere, far off down the base, a horn honked. He could hear something else. There was the sound of men ahead, moving as if engaged in some sort of work.

Across the road there was a gate, set in a fence of steel wire, with the dark face of another warning *No Admittance* sign.

There was darkness beyond, but the gate was open. This was already proof enough that at last he had cornered his man. Johnny drew his service revolver from its holster, moved quietly forward.

His straining eyes now made out the dark outline of a truck parked before the small squat storehouse. He crouched in silence, watching it. He saw a glint of yellow from the doorway of the storehouse, and realized the place was open. Three men came out carrying with difficulty a long yellow box between them. They took it to the truck, pushed it on as if it were very heavy.

Johnny started forward again. He reached the front of the truck, edged around it, gun on the alert.

Then he heard a slight noise behind him. He wheeled, but it was too late. There was a quick rush of air, a muttered voice, and something struck him behind the head with a terrible force. The young Cheyenne fell to the ground, unconscious.

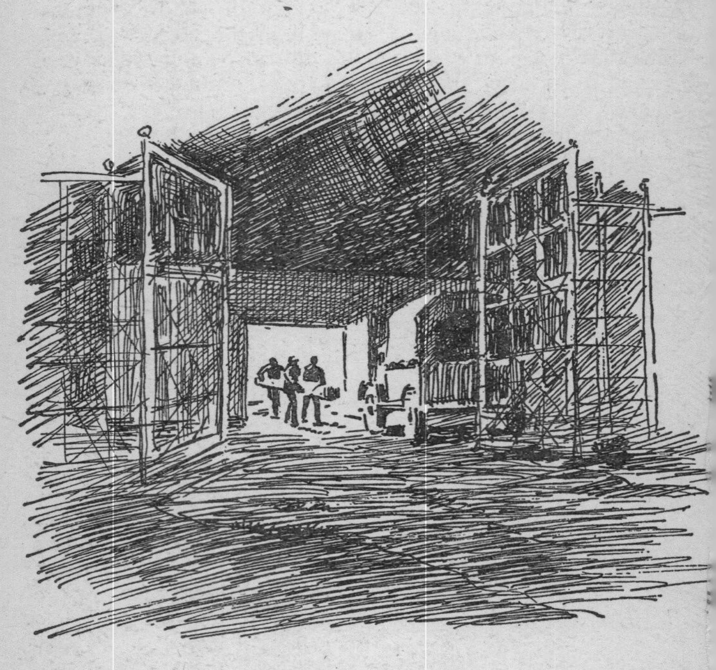

They came out carrying a long yellow box.

Johnny drew his service revolver.

CHAPTER 14

THE MISSING ASTRONAUT

WHEN Mike Mars woke up on that Sunday morning, he was not aware that anything strange had happened while he had slept. He washed and dressed as usual, then went to bang on Johnny's door, singing out, "Ready for chow, Johnny?"

When there was no answer, he banged harder. Johnny oversleep? Even though it was Sunday, his friend was not one to lie abed just lazying. Mike tried the door but it was locked.

Jack Lannigan and Rod Harger came out of their rooms, also dressed and ready to breakfast. "What's with our friend Johnny?" asked the young Navy pilot. "Choose today to catch up on his snoozing?"

Mike shook his head. "He must have gotten up early and gone out. Maybe he took an early morning hike."

"He can have it," grunted Rod. "It's darned cold out mornings here."

"Let's go up and eat," said Mike. "Maybe he'll join us there."

So the three left the quarters and strode up the hill to the officers' club, swinging their arms and breathing deep the crisp mountainy air of that morning. There was no program scheduled that day, even though the big trial of the X-15 was coming the next morning.

Mike had studied and trained and worked over the mastery of the first spaceship until he was trimmed to a high pitch of keenness. It was the opinion of Dr. Holderlin—also shared unanimously by Colonel Drummond, Kent Scott and all the others—that he should set his mind aside from all thoughts and concerns of the next day's trials.

Nevertheless the strange absence of Johnny Bluehawk bothered Mike as he went in for breakfast. This sort of thing had never happened before. Of course, it could have been some sort of emergency—maybe even a family matter, a call during the night.

Even as the three astronauts were pitching into their eggs and bacon, Colonel Drummond was hurriedly putting on his jacket, leaving his own half-finished breakfast on the table, and racing out to a waiting car. He'd had a most alarming phone call from headquarters, and as the car sped him toward his objective his mind was filled with disturbing thoughts.

Reaching the main building, he practically collided with Dr. Holderlin also obviously rushing to the same meeting. The two of them went in together, went on up to the commander's office.

The news the two men, charged with leadership of Space Task Group Q, received there was most disturbing. The officer of the day, the security chief of the base, other Air Force officers, were silent as the two men digested the news.

Sometime during the night a storehouse on the edge of the base had been broken into—no, not really broken into, for it had been *unlocked*—and certain military equipment stolen.

What was missing was a case of ground-to-air missiles, deadly Sidewinder anti-aircraft rockets, and a portable launcher.

This was no ordinary pilfering, for it was not possible for just one man to take these things. It had been a carefully planned job. There were the tracks of a light truck. The footprints of at least three or maybe four men, and worst of all, the key to the storehouse had been in the possession of the thieves, for it was found lying on the ground near the entrance.

Most incriminating though—and the only evidence pointing to the identity of the marauders—was a service revolver lying on the ground as if it had fallen from one of the men in the truck. It had not been fired but it carried the service number of a weapon that had been isued to one of Colonel Drummond's astronauts!

Colonel Drummond wiped his brow. "Impossible. Every one of those boys is absolutely clean. They are good, highly intelligent, they had perfect records. Why would any of them do such a thing?"

Dr. Holderlin muttered, *"Ja,* I think that is impossible. You must be mistaken."

The security chief shook his head. "I'm sorry, gentlemen, but the evidence is plain. The revolver in question was in the possession of your Johnny Bluehawk. It has fingerprints on it, on which we are now awaiting identification. Further, Lieutenant Bluehawk was present in base operations yesterday with no clearly defined objective. It must have been at that time that the opportunity presented itself to take the keys of the storehouse."

As Colonel Drummond was opening his mouth to object, the officer raised a hand to silence him. "Further," he went on, "let me point out that from the beginning of your project, from the very beginning, there has been evidence of interference, sabotage, deliberate trouble making. You have always thought this came from the outside. Let me say that it might just as well have been one of the men on the inside. It might just as well have been this very Bluehawk whose blunder last night has given him away."

"*Nein, nein,*" said Dr. Holderlin. "Not Johnny, never."

The chief of security shrugged a shoulder. "Let me inform you that this Bluehawk did not return to his quarters last night. A check made just a half hour ago revealed his absence and the fact that his bed was not slept in last night."

The phone rang. There was a brief conversation, and the security officer hung up, his eyes were grim. "That was Washington, gentlemen. They have identified the fingerprints on that revolver. They were, indeed, those of your missing astronaut."

Colonel Drummond stood up. "Well, you must search for him. I am sure there is a different story behind this case, but what it is we shall have to learn. Meanwhile, I am going ahead with the X-15 flight tomorrow. We shall keep the news from the rest of the base and especially from the other members of Project Quicksilver. My pilot, Mike Mars—Lieutenant Samson—must not know of this. He must have a clear mind for his visit to outer space."

The meeting broke up. But the alarm that had been set off did not stop in that room. Like the ripples of a pool following the dropping of a rock, the alert was spread.

Anyone seen answering to the description of Johnny Bluehawk—a slim, black-haired, dark-eyed, sharp-nosed young man of American Indian blood—was to be apprehended if he could not identify himself. Outside the base a warning was given to police authorities, in California, Nevada, Utah, and Arizona—look for this man. Why he was wanted was not stated, but all law authorities were warned, find him, hold him, call the Air Force.

Colonel Drummond found the three other astronauts finishing breakfast. As he strode in, he forced a smile on his face and came up to them pretending a good humor he did not feel.

"They have identified the fingerprints."

Mike Mars looked at him, wondered what occasioned this turn.

The colonel sat down as they were finishing up. "Sorry about your friend Johnny," he said, "but we had a special mission for him and had to get him during the night." Anxiously he looked at the three, wondering if perhaps the young Cheyenne might have hinted to any of them of something different. But the look of relief on their faces showed that they had themselves been wondering about Johnny.

"When you see him tomorrow, he'll tell you all about it. Meanwhile, this is Sunday and we want you to forget all about this rocket ship stuff for today. I've got a car and a chauffeur lined up for you outside, and you are going to have a nice ride into Los Angeles this morning, eat a good lunch at some fancy restaurant, see a show or a movie, and be driven back in style after a good restful holiday."

"Yowee!" said Mike, "that's great."

"Yep," chimed in Jack Lannigan. "No flying for today. I'd enjoy a good drive through Southern California greenery today —it'd be a real relief after this desert."

So the three piled out, piled into the Air Force limousine the colonel had for them, and went off for a day's fun.

As for the colonel and Dr. Holderlin, there was no rest for them. Although there was no news of the missing astronaut, and the trail of the thieves' truck had been lost somewhere on the main highway beyond the base, that Sunday was a day of tension.

CHAPTER 15

MISSILE CARGO

JOHNNY BLUEHAWK became aware of a bouncing, jouncing motion. He was in darkness and somewhere in his dreaming he had visions of nightmares, of terror and pain, and of a faintly gleaming building under a moonless star-strewn sky. He moaned, tried to turn in his sleep but something held him.

As he gradually returned to his senses, he heard the rumble of a heavy engine and the sound of tires on a road. He stopped his struggling against the nightmare that seemed to be holding him helpless, and allowed his senses to fully recover. He remembered now creeping up on the strangers at the storehouse, he remembered the truck and then . . . nothing.

Someone must have struck him from behind. Yes, the thought came to him. But then . . . where was he? He opened his eyes.

But nothing registered. He was in a dark place, a moving, rushing dark place. He tried to rise, but could not. His head throbbed from the spot where he had been struck. His hands he found were tied, his feet likewise. He was lying on his side in the dark interior of a truck, wedged against a long box and some roped down machinery. The space inside was narrow and closed, but through the faint crack of the backboards he saw only more darkness and then once the faint flash as of a distant headlight.

It was still night. He had been tied, thrust with the stolen cargo and his captors were heading off through the night. Where? He tried to call out, but found now that the foul taste in his mouth was a rag, tied across his face, keeping him from talking. He was a prisoner. His head throbbed.

He passed out again in pain and weariness. He recalled later several times when he must have regained consciousness. The truck evidently was traveling at high speed all through the night. He recalled once hearing voices talking in the cab—there were three men riding there he determined.

He was fully conscious when the truck finally made a stop. It was early morning and the sun was rising as his captors let down the back of the truck, climbed in and carried him out, still tied helplessly. He saw that they had pulled in behind a ranchlike house somewhere in what must have been the outskirts of a large community. The two men carried him into the back door of the ranch, dumped him on an old cot in one of the rooms and left him.

He spent the day there. During this time, he was fed a couple times, let up once under guard, but his questions were not answered. He caught glimpses of Cahoon several times talking in quiet tones in a front room with the three men who had been driving the truck. Listening carefully with the keen ear of his early outdoor training he heard more than they ever intended.

He had plenty of time to piece together what he had overheard. Gradually he gathered a picture of what was being planned.

From the length of the drive during the night he had suspected they were in the vicinity of Las Vegas, Nevada, and a chance remark or two verified his suspicions. For a moment he wondered whether he could get loose or raise attention, for he knew a little about Las Vegas. Nellis Air Force Base, where he had received his jet training, was just outside that city. There would be Air Force police on patrol in the city. If he could reach them . . . He never suspected that by that morning they too were anxious to reach him.

Cahoon had driven ahead of the truck in his own car. Now they were hiding during the day, waiting for night and the coolness that came with it, to drive on. They were going on somewhere ahead, far up into northern Nevada. He finally caught the name Ely.

Ely . . . why that was the location of the first of the NASA telemetry stations along the X-15's high range! What was Cahoon up to at Ely?

Then he remembered the Sidewinder and the launcher. He shook his head to himself. He couldn't believe it. But he felt sick at heart for he knew no other reason. Cahoon—why Cahoon must be planning to shoot down the X-15 itself!

He set to work even harder to find a way out of his bonds. But they were tight, tied by experts. Cahoon had gathered a group of hardened ruthless criminals, the riffraff of the streets, desperate men who would do anything for pay, in whom there could be no final spark of patriotism.

He knew this for when he was ungagged and allowed food,

The Ely station.

he tried to probe his captors' feelings on acting against their country's own defenders. He got only a blank stare and a curse.

By nightfall, the men had rested. At the coming of darkness, the truck was rolled out of its hiding place, Johnny was carried helplessly back into the truck, and stowed away as before. Cahoon drove off. The three men piled into the cab and another long night drive was on.

This time the truck was stopped at least twice along the road. Johnny, who had been half-dozing, heard the sound of motorcycles and questioning. But whatever forged pass or faked papers Cahoon had supplied his men were effective.

Although Johnny was hoping each time the patrols would search the back of the truck, they never did, but allowed it to go on.

As the night rolled on and the truck bounced and roared its way north along the lonely highways across the vast, sparsely inhabited barrens that is Nevada, Johnny worked steadily at his bonds. He stretched his hands, fought to loosen the cords. Finally he worked himself into a position where he could rub his wrists against a corner of the metal container holding the missiles. Back and forth, just wearing away the strands.

He could sense that dawn was not far away by the time the bonds on his wrists suddenly parted. He rubbed his hands to restore circulation, reached up, untied the gag. He sat up, worked on the cords tying his legs.

Now, hope was racing through him. If he could get clear before his captors could find him—they had looked back into the cab once or twice during the night to check on him—if he could get clear . . .

The cords were tight and difficult. Finally, with raw fingers and chafed hands, shivering in the chill of the high desert air, he freed his legs. He got to his knees, worked his way to the back, peered through the crack in the tailboards.

A faint pink was coloring the horizon. Day was coming. He saw a sign go past, caught the number—*Highway 93 and 50.* From the sunshine behind the truck, they were heading west. That means they must be near Ely—he recalled air maps of his training days. And as he peered out, he saw the first shacks that marked the aproach of habitation.

He worked on the back of the truck. Finally, he forced part of the tailgate open, just enough to allow his body to squeeze through.

The truck slowed for a turn in the road and Johnny seized the opportunity. He pushed through, jumped. He hit the road hard, rolled over several times, and slid into a ditch beside the highway.

When he picked himself up, a little shaken and breathless, the truck was already a good distance away and picking up speed again. His escape had not been noticed.

He set out on foot in the direction the truck had gone, for he must be near the town of Ely.

He walked tired and dusty but with grim determination for a half hour before he came in sight of the little town. Nevada could be a terrifying and rugged state, and Ely was smack in the heart of its most desolate and fearful region. It was high up, surrounded by the semi-barren sides of sloping ancient and eroded mountains. On all sides stretched the wastes of what had once been called the Great American Desert. There was mining here, there were still ranches given over to sheep raising on the stumpy grass and the scattered trees of this land.

Ely was a collection of scattered houses, with a booming attempt at a main street. At night, as Johnny trudged along its deserted sidewalk, he could imagine ranchers and miners whooping it up in the several night spots, gambling halls, and drinking parlors that gave it still a touch of the Old West. But now the town was still asleep in the first rays of the dawning sun, its lights dark, a few cars parked silently on the street, the chill of the mountain morning still lingering.

Johnny found the office of the deputy sheriff on a little street just off the main stem. He banged on the door. He banged again. Finally he heard a stomping noise, and a man opened the door.

Obviously just awakened, the man had hastily slung a jacket with the deputy's badge pinned on it over his pajamas. He was a paunchy, middle-aged man, balding, with gray-tinged handle-bar mustaches in obvious imitation of the oldtime sheriffs.

"Whut can I do fer you, son?" he said, looking at Johnny Bluehawk curiously. He saw his wrinkled, dusty, Air Force uniform, looked sharply now at his visitor's coppery features. He stood aside. "Come in and set a spell, Lieutenant," he said then.

Johnny slipped inside, fell into an armchair at the side of the sheriff's roll-top desk. "Gosh," he said. "Am I glad to see you. You've got to get word back for me at once."

"That's right, young feller," said the deputy, reaching up and taking down his belt and holstered revolver from the wall and buckling it on. "That's exactly what I aim to do. Just wait there a minute till I get back. I got to attend to somethin'."

He left and closed the door behind him. Johnny leaned back wearily. He heard the sound of the deputy sheriff in the hall, heard the noise of a telephone being cranked, heard the whisper of a voice as the deputy was saying something low.

He frowned. That was odd, for there was a telephone of a standard type right on the lawman's desk. Johnny, with quick suspicion, got up, put his ear to the door.

"That's him all right," said the voice of the deputy. "This is the very feller the Air Force wants to get their hands on. Dangerous, the message I got says. Come over and bring the other fellers. I'll try to hold him till we can get him into the jail."

Johnny was startled. He glanced around, looked in the deputy's desk. There was a scribbled message lying in plain sight. He read it. It was a description of himself—hold this man, dangerous, possible saboteur—if you catch him, notify the Air Force police and keep him *incommunicado*. That meant nobody was to talk to him, nobody was to be allowed to hear what he had to say.

Johnny realized that the security of Project Quicksilver was behind this, but he had to get his message off at once. The X-15 was in danger!

He jumped quickly to the window, raised it quietly. He could hear the voice of the deputy apparently calling other members of his posse. He slipped a foot over it, slipped out into the narrow alley, raced off down it.

There was a car parked at the far end, along another street. He reached the car, it was unlocked, the key was in the ignition. Who locks cars in a place like Ely?

He climbed in, started the engine. As he did so, he caught a glimpse of the deputy sheriff leaning out of the window. "Hey!" the man called, and then began to wave his pistol. But the young Cheyenne stepped on the gas and barreled the old car down the dusty side street.

Johnny raced for the car.

CHAPTER 16

X-15 COUNTDOWN

MIKE MARS bounced out of bed full of pep that Monday morning. He had been awakened exactly at daybreak by a knock on his door from one of the men on duty in the quarters. It was much earlier than he'd been arising before, but the Sunday off, the day in the city, had been like a real tonic to him. He knew he'd have had more fun if Johnny Bluehawk could have been along with them, but still Mike had made the most of the day's rest. The strain of study, the routine of work, had been broken. He was raring to go.

It had not been a day of rest for the other men at the Air Force Flight Test Center that day—those of them involved in the X-15 project. For the countdown prior to the big flight had started in the middle of Sunday and had gone on all through the night. It would end only when the moment of action came.

While Mike and Jack and Rod had been enjoying themselves in Los Angeles, the hangars had been a beehive of activity. The checking of the X-15 had been carefully undertaken. Its operating system gone over systematically so that nothing would go amiss that could humanly be corrected. This process was not one that could be done simply in a few minutes, nor would anyone have wanted to just brush it off.

The B-52 mother plane, too, was just as rigorously checked. Men climbed about the huge plane testing circuits, examining valves, tracing lines. Then the process of connecting the tiny rocket plane to the underside of the big bomber's wing had been gone through. The little plane had been rolled over, jacked up, and mechanics worked over the strong clamps that linked it tightly to the B-52's system.

In the early hours of the morning, the trucks rolled up and the process of servicing the two ships' fuel tanks and auxiliary systems began. The gases which would enable Mike to breathe during flight were pumped in, checked and rechecked—oxygen for life, nitrogen for pressure. The auxiliary tanks for these in the B-52 similarly serviced.

Next the cooling and ventilation system tanks in the X-15 were serviced, the volatile hydrogen peroxide, the steaming liquid nitrogen, helium, water and alcohol systems prepared.

As Mike, Jack, and Rod parked Mike's quaint old Ford near the hangar and walked around, the sun still only just rising in the sky, the scene that greeted their eyes looked truly strange.

The huge plane stood there and at first sight they had the impression that its right wing must have been burning, for it seemed surrounded by a swirling cloud of white smoke.

But there was no smoke smell nor had Mike expected any. As he came closer to the scene, he could see the outlines of the tank trucks and the figures of curiously cloaked and masked men bending over the shadowy fog-encircled body of the X-15 now hanging beneath the wide wing above it.

The fog was the artificial mist caused by the evaporation of the main fuels that would propel the rocket plane. The liquid oxygen was being pumped in.

Liquid oxygen was air-reduced to such a terrible degree of cold that it becomes a liquid like water, a liquid which can be pumped and stored and burned like gasoline. But the cold was so intense that even the chill of the morning air in the Mojave must have had the effect of a blast of boiling heat, for boiling away was just what the frozen air was doing.

As the lines pumped the violent fuel into the X-15's great tank space, frost formed on everything the frigid liquid came in contact with and the vapor of its boiling surface sent a man-made fog wrapping its arms around the whole area.

Mike stood aside and watched as the tanks were filled. Another truck was topping the extra tanks in the body of the B-52. All through the flight up and out to the moment of launching this liquid gas would be sizzling away, boiling itself off. The mother ship would carry an additional supply to replace what was lost before launching.

Colonel Drummond caught sight of Mike and the two other young pilots. He hurried over to them, called them together. In a corner of the hangar were gathered the other men who would be flying in this venture. Major Coppard, commander aboard the B-52, shook hands briefly with Mike and slapped him on the back.

"We're going to make it up there, today, eh?" he laughed.

"You bet," said Mike. "I'm ready when you are."

"Enough, enough," said Drummond, who seemed a little tense, more so than Mike had seen him before. For him the past twenty-four hours had been no rest, he had had little sleep that night too.

There then followed a quick briefing of the day's plans. Mike knew it by heart, as did all the men, but they went through it again. There was only one change from their previous plans. Bluehawk—"still away on special duty" according to Drummond's hasty aside—would be replaced in one of the chase planes. These two planes would be manned by Lannigan and Harger instead.

"I'm going to be in the B-52," said Drummond, "but strictly as an observer. Once we're off the ground, Coppard is in control until the drop."

The briefing party broke up. The men of the B-52 returned to their plane, climbed up into their various places.

The van was alongside the ship now, and Mike went over to it, was helped up the ladder to the back and the doors shut. Once inside, he found the pressure suit waiting. He was still in a good mood and was joking with the attendants as they fitted the space suit on him, but he gave a gasp when he saw the helmet they had prepared for him. Instead of having hastily scribbled letters on the white helmet front, they had very

"That's for luck, sir."

neatly lettered his initials, M.A.R.S., there and above it a tiny circle with a diagonal arrow—the astronomic symbol of the planet Mars.

"That's for luck, sir," said one of the men, as he adjusted the helmet over Mike's grinning freckled face.

"Can't miss," said Mike. They tightened the helmet down, checked the fittings. "See you later, boys," said Mike as he made his way down the ladder and across to the X-15.

Here he was helped up into the tight space of the cockpit-cabin. Once in, the canopy was snapped down, and he sealed it from the inside.

He started his ventilation system. The rocket ship was now closed off.

There was a rumbling sound. Mike glanced out. The B-52 and its burden were now being towed out to the field.

As the big plane was put into position to start its engines, Rod and Jack were already seated in the cockpits of their F-100 chase planes and going through their own check ups. Systematically, they went through the routines with their ground crew men that would guarantee their own safety.

This completed, their canopies were swung shut, and they were ready.

The B-52's mighty jets came to life, one after the other. When they were roaring away, Mike, whose earphones kept him directly in touch with everything going on aboard the bomber, heard Coppard going through the cockpit check in the nose of the jet.

When that was completed, Coppard's voice came to Mike. "Ready for cockpit check?"

Mike snapped his yes, and they proceeded to the same routine for the captive rocket ship.

As the B-52 rolled under its own power to the start of its runway, the two chase planes speeded up, raced on down the field and kicked off. Up they went, as if to herald the rising of the monster.

Then Coppard pushed on the power. The huge Boeing bomber rolled faster and faster down the long runway and then it too was airborne.

The planes rose to 38,000 feet, about seven miles high above the barren wastes of the Mojave. Turning their noses northeast they roared away in the direction of Wendover, Utah, 485 miles away.

At the speed they flew they reached it in less than an hour.

They did not put down, instead the B-52 circled around, started back as if to return directly to Edwards.

They crossed the entire state of Nevada, they had come along the track of the high range, they had passed over the NASA telemetry stations at Beatty and Ely.

As they had done so, Mike had briefly heard the acknowledgments of these stations. Within them, over consoles and radar dials, men were watching everything that was going on. He knew they could tell more about him in his ship than the dials on his own cockpit could tell him.

He wondered oddly for a moment as he heard the voice of Frank Moultrie checking in at Ely to advise that everything was shipshape there whether Frank could say as much for what was going on outside his door.

Mike admired the efficiency of the radar trackers but this other thought amused him. He knew they worked in closed rooms, with their accesses to the outside limited to the electronic contacts of their radar and emissions. But probably they couldn't tell what was going on just outside their closed doors. A coyote and its cubs could be prowling their outer hall for food and they'd never know it.

He returned his attention to his cockpit, dropping the thought.

It was curiously prophetic as to what in fact was going on just outside Frank Moultrie's mountain top station.

"Topping your tanks," said Coppard's voice. Mike acknowledged. The B-52 was now transferring new amounts of liquid oxygen into his main tank to replace that part of which had fizzed away during the time which had passed. Mike called out the readings on his fuel gauge, until again it registered *Full*.

The chase planes called in to acknowledge that everything seemed shipshape. The observers in the B-52, who could watch the captive X-15 from closed-circuit television eyes at front and rear acknowledged that all seemed in order.

"Twelve minutes," called Coppard's voice. Mike acknowledged, read the gauges on his cockpit, checked his windshield nitrogen setting.

Then, soon enough, came the next countdown call, "Eight minutes."

"Pressure cooling."

"On," said Mike calmly.

"Jettison switches."

"Off," came Mike's report.

Radar at Ely

"Seven minutes . . . Nitrogen bleed."
"On."
"Chamber pressure."
"Preheat."
"On."
"Data reading . . ."
"Six minutes."
"Pressurized."
"Data on."
"On and calibrating."
"Five minutes."
"Auxiliary Pressure Unit On."
"Hydraulic pressure, electric power—check."
"Four minutes . . ."
"Three minutes."
"Check controls, rudder, lateral . . ."
"Launch light."
"On."

Mike felt himself calm. He went through the routine count-down just as he had many times before in the simulator and before the glide drop. He felt that cool, a little bit out-of-it-all feeling that always came over him in moments of crisis. He was ready.

"One minute warning," came Coppard's equally cool voice.

"Engine master switch."

"On," said Mike, flicking it.

"Prime switches . . . on."

Mike reached out, turned on his master switch. In his ear-phones, he heard a faint cough, then Coppard began counting:

"Five, four, three, two, one . . .

"Drop!"

CHAPTER 17

ON THE WARPATH

As Johnny Bluehawk's stolen car took him down the early morning streets of Ely, he could sense that behind him the authorities of the town were rapidly coming to life. He saw a man getting into a car along the same street but fortunately the man, carrying a rifle, did not know that his quarry was already escaping town.

He drove desperately and while he drove figured his plan of action. The saboteurs with their anti-aircraft missile would be heading up the mountain, going up to the telemetry station outside Ely. It would be the only place they could be sure that the X-15 would pass directly over; it was high up; they had a chance of hitting it with their powerful missile if they could catch it before its rise. It was a matter of split-second timing.

Since Johnny had failed to enlist the aid of Ely's police, nothing was left to him but to try to stop the plot himself. If time permitted, he could at least warn the men in the tracker station and they could warn the X-15 and its mother ship.

Where was the station? He was out of town now, and heading into the high mountains that ringed the little community. It was about ten miles out of town on the highest peak. Abruptly the paved highway stopped.

His question was answered at the same time. Beyond the end of the pavement a narrower dirt-packed road ran curving up the steep mountainside. A sign posted at its beginning warned all persons that they were entering upon United States property and no trespassing.

Unhesitantly Johnny turned the old car up the path, and started along it. The road was not too steep, winding around and around through thick underbrush, broken country, barren areas and stands of pine.

It was a narrow road through, certainly not enough for two cars. Johnny looked back, as he turned a curve and far below he could see the roofs of Ely and a rising trail of dust that must have been the automobiles of the pursuing sheriff's posse. He realized that his own car was throwing up a trail of dust behind it. They could see exactly where their quarry was.

He remembered they had rifles and that they were mountain men, born and bred to this country. They could possibly cut around him, might know short cuts, might even be able to pick him off, especially if they had better cars. Certainly this old jalopy he was driving, now wheezing from the climb and the altitude, was hardly one to give a man confidence.

Johnny braked the car, swerved it across until it blocked the road. He shut off the engine, climbed out. He'd escape into the brush, make his way on foot the rest of the route. The posse would have to follow the road now that his dust cloud trail had stopped. They would find the car, they'd have to go on foot themselves, spread out, search for him.

While they were so occupied, he could be making his own way directly up to the station. He reached back in the car, removed a tire iron from the back seat—this was a weapon.

He began his climb. Upward he toiled, running and leaping rocks, moving fast. He felt himself becoming hot in the rising morning sun, despite the thinness of the mountain air. He stopped, caught his breath. Suddenly a thin-lipped smile broke his face. He remembered the games and lore of his childhood, the days on the reservation of the dwindling but still proud Northern Cheyennes.

This cold high air was like home to him. This landscape was one he knew. He stripped off his jacket, his undershirt. He removed his service shoes, stood in his bare feet, naked from the waist up. He took the little blue feather he carried in his wallet for good luck—that he'd always carried since his father had given it to him on the night of his tribal manhood ceremony, and inserted it in his hair, twisting a tiny clump to hold it. He rubbed two streaks of yellowish, clayey dirt across his cheeks, and gave a short sharp yell, the whoop of the Cheyenne on the warpath.

Now he raced on, renewed in spirit, fighting keen, waiting to close in on his foe. His coppery figure, swiftly moving feet, covered ground. In his hand he swung the tire iron, sorry he had nothing to decorate it with.

Somewhere below him he heard cars squeal to a halt. The posse must have reached his stalled car. He didn't flicker a smile—he had a good lead.

It still took the better part of an hour to make the top of the mountain on foot, but Johnny was equipped for it. He moved tirelessly in the manner of his boyhood exercises, and his sharp eyes picked out the best paths upward, avoiding the road which ran several hundred feet away.

Finally he was on top. Far away in all directions lay a breath-taking landscape. A desolate awesome area of jumbled mountains, barren dry lakes, scrub, ridges and valleys. Just beyond the 9000-foot peak the glistening yellowish surface of Jakes Dry Lake could be seen in the valley beyond, with mountains on its far side. This was another emergency landing spot for experimental planes, Johnny knew.

Before him he could see the low one-storey concrete building of the NASA tracking station, with its big metal ear of a radar atop its far corner, looking over the expanse. Beyond that, on the ledge just before the drop off down the other side of the mountain was the weird telemeter antenna, like some futuristic gun—a long rod wound around with twisting wire and set with a mesh collar.

He crouched as he saw the truck parked by the station, saw the far-off forms of the men who had held him captive. They were wheeling the portable rocket launcher over to the ledge, setting it up to overlook the scene, to span the skies where the X-15 would pass in a matter of a few minutes more.

Johnny knew that the time was close. He had been estimating the hours of that morning and he knew the schedule. Cahoon and his men could not have gone about their work on the ledge in plain view of the station were it not that the small crew manning the station were already at their posts, before the consoles of their electronic equipment, heedless and mindless of what was doing beyond their door.

He ran lightly forward, trying to keep under cover and yet not to waste time. He came to the little guard house by the side of the road entering the grounds. There should have been a guard stationed here. He slipped up to it, glanced in.

There had indeed been a guard there, and the truck men had taken him before he could give an alarm. He was lying now, on the floor of the cabin, hands tied, and obviously unconscious.

But there was no time to rescue him. Johnny heard one of Cahoon's men call out from the far ledge. The planes must be in sight.

Throwing caution to the winds, Johnny grasped the tire iron hard, and sprinted across the hard dirt of the cleared mountain top. He passed the truck, he ran by the station itself.

Cahoon and two of his men were lifting a Sidewinder missile, setting it up in the launcher. They were not looking his way.

Johnny raced on silently. The missile slid into place, and Cahoon stepped back. As he did so, he looked up and his face registered shock. He saw an Indian warrior charging at him.

The two others spotted him at the same time. "Holy smokes!" shouted one, and jumped away, reaching for a pistol, but Johnny hurled the iron. It struck the man full across the face and he fell like a stoned rabbit.

The second man jumped aside, began to run for the truck. Cahoon cursed, leaped for Johnny and the two met.

Johnny's flashing fist thudded against Cahoon's chest. Then the two grappled, struggled back and forth, rolling over and over on the ground. Cahoon was swearing, desperate. Johnny was equally furious, and as he rolled he was yelling threats in the Cheyenne language of his fathers.

Now Cahoon gave a yell, slipped from Johnny's grasp, got to his feet. The Indian lunged for him, but Cahoon stepped away, ran toward the Sidewinder.

Johnny dashed after him. Again they met and struggled on their feet, as Cahoon tried again and again to reach the launching button of the rocket missile. The Sidewinder was a deadly hunter of flying planes. A powerful solid-fuel rocket, nine feet long yet only five inches in diameter, weighing but the same as a heavy man, it could reach a speed two and a half times that of sound. It could travel eight miles on its own rocket thrust, it carried a high-explosive warhead, and what made it so deadly was that it hungered for the heat of an airplane exhaust. Its remarkable infra-red guidance system infallibly directed it to the nearest source of heat radiation—and when launched toward an airplane, especially a jet plane, the Sidewinder would turn itself, direct itself at that heat source until it met and blew itself up in the moment of impact.

Faster than any fighter jet, faster than any bomber, once fixed on its prey, none could escape.

Though neither Johnny nor his antagonist had time to look up, the B-52 was separating. A tiny black splinter had dropped off its wing, nearly over the Ely station, and a tiny spark of fire shot from the splinter's rear.

Following the black splinter's course came two silvery Super Sabres, far up, faintly visible.

Cahoon broke free, slammed his hand on the launching button, then dropped to hit the ground.

Cahoon saw an Indian warrior.

The fighting Cheyenne saw the spurt of flame from the Sidewinder, jumped aside too to protect himself.

There was a hiss, a roar of rocket thunder and the long white rocket raced up into the sky, raced on its own jet of fire, raced up to hunt for itself a haven of heat in the sky—a spot of warmth in which it could happily shatter itself to shreds and thereby fulfill its only reason for existence.

CHAPTER 18

THE STARS BY DAY

THE MOMENT he heard the word "drop," Mike's fingers turned the launching switch on. There was a sudden instant of fall as the plane fell free from the wing of the Stratofortress, for a split-second moving along with it on the same momentum. Without hesitation, Mike's trained left hand thrust in the throttle.

Instantly he felt himself pushed back against his seat—not too powerfully for he had at first put the engines on at their lowest capabilities. But he knew that behind the little black dart-shaped ship was now a lancing jet of vicious flame, a jet that must be as long as his ship.

It felt at first the way a powerful jet pilot feels when he first kicks on full power. Mike felt confident then, knew he could handle it.

The X-15 had already pulled away from the big jet bomber, was already accelerating on its thrust of burning gases. Mike's eyes swept the gauges before him, all was in order.

He slowly stepped up the throttle, adding fuel to the hungry mouth of his powerful rocket engine, the most powerful plane engine ever built by man. Behind the plane the saber of burning flame lengthened.

In his earphones came the crisp words of the chase pilot Jack Lannigan, telling him how he looked, advising him as to the X-15's appearance. Mike spoke softly into his own throat mike, acknowledging, then saying, "I'm taking her up now."

Coppard's voice now flowed in easily, yet Mike could sense the excitement behind it, the fervor that must be possessing everyone aboard the B-52. "O.K. . . ." A pause, then, "Give our regards to the stars."

Mike smiled briefly, brought the nose of the X-15 up. It responded fast and sweet. The black rocket ship now almost directly above the Ely tracker station, turned tail down to the Earth below, and headed for the heavens in a high steep climb.

Mike advanced the power, more and more. As he did so he

felt himself being forced back into his seat by the rising acceleration. He breathed deeply, imagining himself back in the centrifuge during a routine test. He had imagined this flight so often, that at first the real thing seemed like just another trial. His eyes, beginning to pain under the strain of the rising G-forces of his swiftly increasing speed, swept the cockpit. Everything in order, working perfectly.

Somewhere down below other eyes were watching his gauges as well. But now he was in charge. He forced the throttle on to full thrust.

He was back in his seat now, pinned back by a mighty hand that tried to clamp him to his seat, that tried to stifle his breath, to sit on his lungs, to squeeze his heart. His wrists felt encircled by leaden bonds, but he could move his finger by mighty effort.

He strained, and his mind began to sing in defiance. His eyes raised to the thin, tight windows of the rocket ship's tiny cabin saw but the blue of the empty sky ahead of him. The ship was riding a lance of fire now twice the length of the ship. It was rising, rising.

His mind sang defiantly: "Michael Mars is my name . . ."

The speed gauge had passed 1500 miles an hour. He had been rising . . . what . . . just twenty seconds . . .

"America's my nation," Mike murmured through compressed lips and aching teeth. Two thousand miles an hour and adding power. The thrust was great—what now—six times the weight of his own body—no, seven. Seven times his own weight. But not more.

The throttle was on, the furious raging engine was burning up liquid oxygen and ammonia at an insane rate—10,000 pounds a minute flowing down and blasting out. Why, Mike had no time to think but knew from his training, the F-100 can only burn 40,000 pounds in a whole hour at top flight. The lance behind him now, the fiery tail of the man-made rocket must now be a huge insanely brilliant jet, three times the length of the ship.

"Space-flying is my game," he muttered as the needle of his speed gauge touched 3000 miles an hour. That was close to space-flight speed, but not yet. Not this time.

A minute gone by, only a minute? The force, the pressure, made time drag, made him feel as if he could not stand another instant, made him want to scream and yell for help. But he didn't, for he had been through this before and besides, just as his own personal ditty had always insisted ever since he was twelve years old, "And Mars my destination!"

He didn't actually get this out aloud, it would have been too much. In his ringing ears he could hear faintly the voice of Major Coppard relaying the information that the tracking station was telling him. "Everything is in order, the ship is functioning perfectly."

But Mike knew that too. A minute and a half. How far up now? Not more than a small part of the way. The next half minute under full drive, that would do the trick.

He hung on, again feeling calm and cool despite the agony of the 7 G's bearing down on him. Beyond his windows the sky had darkened a little bit, a darker blue and for a flickering instant the thought passed through his mind that it must be nearing nightfall.

But no . . . it was only the air thinning out.

Then the hand of the timer, approaching the two-minute mark. He watched it crawl slowly, second by painful second, toward the line. At last, two minutes, and his left hand, weighted down, forced itself up and thrust the terrible weight of the tiny toggle switch forward.

The engines died. The saber of flame shortened, shortened swiftly, then suddenly blacked out as if sheathed.

Mike felt himself swing forward in his seat, bounce against the restraining straps. He was free of weight. He was out of acceleration, he was falling freely forward on the momentum of the drive. Sixty miles the height gauge registered, sixty miles up and still traveling.

He spoke into his mike, announced the shut-off. "I'm in free fall now, but still rising on course."

"Acknowledge," said a voice, that of Moultrie was it? It was not the B-52 now.

Mike spoke now. "The sky before me is becoming quite dark. It's still blue but a very dark blue and—yes, there are stars out. I can see them breaking through. It's like just after twilight."

He read off his gauges, the voice from below checked with him.

He was still in free fall, would be until the X-15 finally reached the end of its momentum, until its speed of climb would reach zero and the ship would start its drop back to Earth.

The engine had burned out but the thrust left was enough

to carry the X-15 out beyond the atmosphere, up over one hundred miles from the surface of the world of men.

It seemed to Mike that the sky darkened even as he talked. Now more stars were appearing, and more, and then it became almost totally black, like the blackest of moonless nights.

He was in space and he thrilled through and through. He had made it, he was the first to reach outer space, the first to venture across the threshold of the greatest frontier before humanity.

He took control of the plane now. There were the compressed air rocket tubes in the wings and tail. He guided the ship onto its curve, bringing it around slowly in a giant arc so that it could begin the moment of its return under guidance.

As he worked, he talked and described how the stars were so brilliant and sharp and clear. "And there's the Moon," he said. "In its last quarter, down near the horizon. It looks so strange, so cold and sharply defined. It looks," he said, "exactly as if I were using a telescope. I can see the tiny sharp peaks of its mountains and craters in the long shadows of its coming nightfall."

Never had he seen the heavens so sharply. He felt himself filled with awe at the vastness of the universe seen from outside the Earth's warm comforting blanket of air. "It's great out here," he said. "It's just the greatest."

But his speed gauge was saying zero.

The X-15 glided along in a region almost entirely airless, whose thin traces of atmosphere were less than a thousandth the pressure down on the surface. It began to dip, under Mike's control, and gently he turned its nose down in a long easy glide back to Earth.

Now for the first time he saw the world he had left, could see it through his cockpit windows. It was a vast wonderful glowing panorama, bright in sunlight. It was a mass of tans and browns and reddish tinges, with areas of greenish-gray, and a blinding mirrorlike flash of dazzling blue that was the Pacific Ocean. He saw the western coast of the North American continent outlined as on a very realistic relief map and he could see the outlines of Mexico and right up to the coastline of Vancouver and the Canadian Yukon.

For a dazzling second his eyes rested on the sun itself—a blinding white ball against the black sky, with the awe-inspiring luminous arms of its fantastic corona rising hundreds of thousands of miles beyond the sun's flaming surface. And, visible, even around the sun itself, the millionfold stars of the galaxy that was waiting the advent of Man the Conqueror. But the time for sight-seeing had run out. . . .

Mike was busy once more, for he was again out of free fall. He was braced in his seat against the forces of deceleration, the rising pressure of the X-15's slowing down as it encountered the rapid rise of the Earth's atmosphere.

Again he was subjected to intense discomfort, but the pressure of his bodily weight was not his main concern. Anxiously he was watching the temperature gauges, those that told of the heat on the ship's skin as well as the heat in his cabin.

Inside all was in order. The ship's superb air-conditioning mechanism was meeting the demands placed upon it fully.

Outside the temperature was rising rapidly. He held the ship to as gentle an incline as possible, he tried to delay its glide down so that it could ease into the blanket of air with the least friction.

For it would be the friction of that air against his hull, falling at ever increasing speed, that would be the moment of the X-15's ultimate test. Everything else that had gone before could have been predicted. But could it hold together under the heat—the melting heat?

The outside skin was hot, was rising. He saw the tip of the nose turning red, red-hot. He glanced aside and saw the tips of his short wings glowing red, gaining scarlet coloring. The black paint with which the X-15 was coated was specially heat-resistant but it would burn away at a thousand degrees. He held the controls firmly and watched the gauges.

Now there were puffs of smoke past his windows, and he looked outside. The surface of his ship was bubbling! There were wrinkles and bubbles and puffs all over, as if it had suddenly turned old and wrinkled. The paint was burning off.

The gauges showed this, and yet Mike knew that the very act of burning would serve to cool the hard metal shell beneath that paint. Time, time, did he have time?

The ship was widening its glide. Outside the sky's blackness had disappeared, the blue was lightening, lightening.

Mike gritted his teeth. He felt hot. He glanced at his own suit, his own cabin. The heat was winning slowly over the air-conditioning. It was getting warmer within, while without the ship was wreathed in the flames of its burning skin, its red-hot wing tips, its nearly white-hot nose.

This is how a meteor goes, Mike thought, this is how a meteor burns up on hitting the atmosphere. He pulled the ship out flatter, pumped his retro-rockets to hold back the fall.

The perspiration forced its way onto Mike's face, under the protective helmet, under his mask, against the struggling efforts of his suit's conditioning. Not more than one hundred degrees in here, he told himself. Not more than that. I had to expect it.

But now there came a change. The ship was riding smoothly, more smoothly. He saw the sky was blue again, the stars long vanished. The Earth below was near. There was a bouncing sensation, the air was furnishing a surface.

He pulled the stick back, and the wingflaps found resistance, took hold. The pressure eased up sharply, and Mike broke out in a wide sharp smile.

"Got it," he said suddenly.

He heard a long sigh of relief in his earphones. Down below, on three telemetry stations they knew he had pulled out, they knew the heat was going away, they knew the red-hot wings had cooled off, the skin returning to normal, the pilot still alive and safe. The X-15 had come through.

Laughing exultantly, Mike brought the X-15 down closer and closer to the ground. He knew where he was. He had crossed most of Nevada during his climb and fall. He was past the Beatty station, heading for Edwards, heading for home.

He drove the little gliding plane on, now twelve miles from the ground, now ten. Lower and lower, and then he caught sight of a tiny plane far below. He squinted—what a toy plane, he thought, and then chuckled. It was the mighty B-52 still at seven miles height. He came down to its level and the voice of Frank Coppard laughed in his ear.

"Now take her down on Rogers and we'll begin the celebration, spaceman!" said Coppard.

Mike grinned, headed the spaceship turned glider for the now familiar surface configuration of Edwards Field and Rogers Dry Lake.

"Coming in correctly," said another voice. Mike glanced swiftly back. It was one of the chase planes, back on the job. That was Jack Lannigan's voice. He didn't see any sign of Rod Harger's chase plane, though.

"How does the X-15 look now?" asked Mike.

"Ha!" said Lannigan's voice. "You look beautiful to me, feller. Just like something the cat dragged in!"

Mike grinned and began his landing pattern. The first spaceship was coming back down.

CHAPTER 19

SIDEWINDER JUSTICE

ATOP the mountain near Ely, standing just outside the telemetry station, Johnny Bluehawk climbed to his feet. Opposite him, the man called Cahoon also got to his feet. Though a few moments before both men had been in desperate combat, now they stood as if not aware of each other's presence, simply staring up into the sky where a tiny red flame that marked the exhaust of a Sidewinder missile had vanished.

They could not see it, but they knew it was somewhere up there, racing at faster than sound speed toward one of the planes in the sky.

Johnny was sure that it would not be the X-15. For the firing of the missile had been delayed by his struggle. The X-15 was not in sight, but Johnny knew that by now it was heading up into the regions of the upper atmosphere under its own tremendous rocket power. But there was still the Boeing Stratofortress, the B-52 with its four roaring turbojets mounted in the wings. And there were still two F-100 fighter planes in the sky, each with a powerful jet driving it on.

The Sidewinder had to find its source of heat. Nothing else would satisfy it.

Cahoon stared upward, his face tense, a mask of hate and fury. Johnny stared upward, troubled, biting his lip.

They waited, as if in mutual truce, as if dice had been cast that would decide the outcome of their contest. Inside the station, in the closed sound-proofed room of the electronics equipment, Frank Moultrie and his crew were talking and reading records and keeping track of events miles away. They knew and suspected nothing of the things which had occurred outside.

The two other men of Cahoon's gang, the third still unconscious, were already panicked. The two were in the truck, trying to start its engine. As they got it going, ignoring their leader, four cars came chugging and panting up the road, drove into the station. As the cars ground to a halt, a dozen men piled out, carrying rifles and pistols.

There was a scuffle and the two men in the truck surrendered. Then as the posse started to where Johnny and Cahoon were standing, all came to a halt, all lifted their eyes.

There was a puff of black smoke high in the sky. The B-52 swept on. One of the silvery chase planes flew on. But the second chase plane was falling.

The Sidewinder had found its target. It had been much too late for the X-15. It had been too late for the mother ship. But it was right on time for the two Super Sabres. And it picked the one piloted by Rod Harger.

One moment Rod was seated smoothly in his cockpit, his eyes fixed on the disappearing fire track of the X-15 piloted by his hated rival. The next instant he was thrown forward by a tremendous blow, and his ship was whirling end over end downward, its rear blown off.

Rod didn't lose consciousness. He fought the controls, then realized he had nothing to control. He darted his hand out, seized the yellow lever next his seat, pulled. There was an explosion under him, and the seat—pilot and all—went up through the rolled-back canopy, somersaulted through the air.

A parachute bloomed and slowly Rod came floating down the thin Nevada mountain air and settled many minutes later onto the hard flat floor of Jakes Dry Lake.

He broke himself free from his harness, and standing under the pitiless hot sun of the baked desert lake floor, he managed to get off his flying suit. Then he started the long tiresome walk back across the desolate desert floor to Ely.

The men on the mountain top forgot for a moment what they had been doing as they watched the orange parachute flower high in the air. But then they recovered, ran again toward Johnny Bluehawk. Before Johnny could do anything. several men had seized him, thrown him down, were holding him for the deputy sheriff.

"Let me up!" Johnny yelled. "Get the other fellow, he's your man!"

But the posse men shook their heads. The Indian was the fellow the Air Force was looking for and they had him. By the time the sheriff arrived, by the time explanations had been made, by the time Frank Moultrie had been dragged away from his instruments and brought outside, by the time a message to Edwards had cleared Johnny, Cahoon had made good his getaway. He had been held by one of the deputies during their first attack. But he had been fighting with Johnny

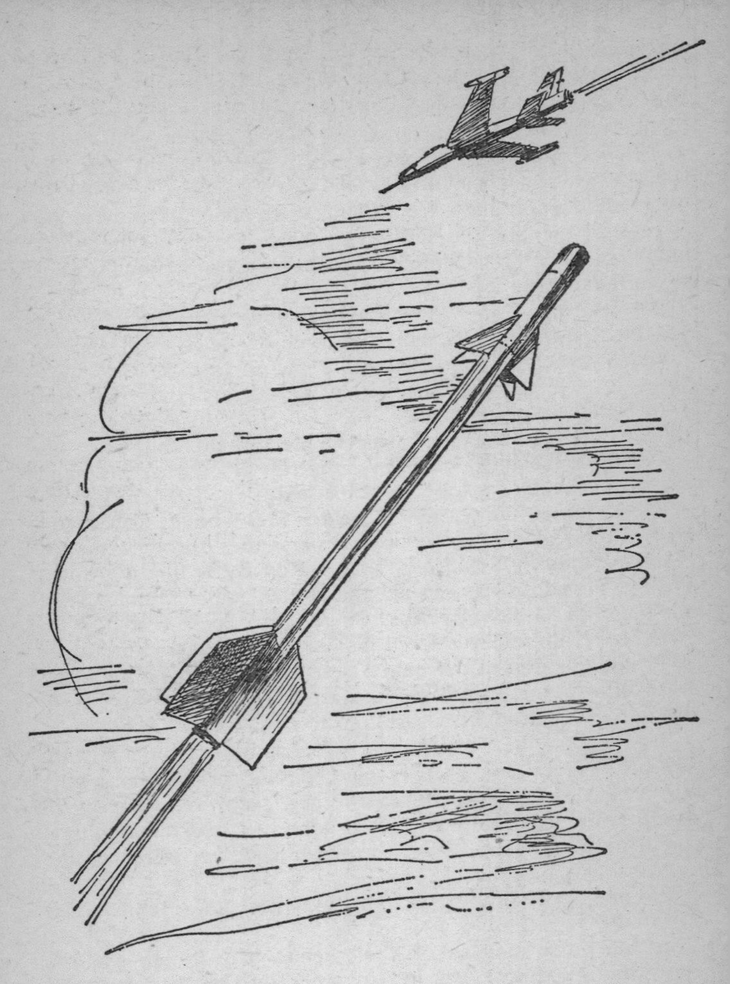

The Sidewinder.

and quickly he had made that deputy think that he had been but an honest defender of the station. This enabled him to twist away, when the deputy was distracted, to slip off down the mountainside.

When they finally were straightened out as to who was who, it was too late. Though the posse spent the rest of the day beating through the bushes, Cahoon was gone.

Late that afternoon the four astronauts finally got together again. Rod had been picked up by a car from Ely, hot, angry, tired, and hailed as a hero "who had deliberately flown his plane into the missile to save the X-15" (which is how one of the posse described it and how they came to think of it). Then he and Johnny had flown back to Edwards with Frank Moultrie when the plane arrived from NASA headquarters after Mike Mars had brought his scorched but triumphant spaceship down safely to Rogers Dry Lake.

Jack Lannigan, of course, brought his chase plane down safe and sound with an eye-witness story worth the telling.

They had quite a celebration that night with everyone joining in. But even as they laughed and sang and described their experiences over and over again, Mike Mars knew that for him this was but the second step up the ladder of space. There was a third step and more to come. That third step was waiting for him over on the east coast, at the place that has been called Spaceport, U.S.A., or Earthstrip One—Cape Kennedy. There were already giant rockets waiting there, on one of which he would voyage again into outer space.

The story of Mike Mars at Cape Kennedy and of that moment when he rode a raging Redstone rocket to the edge of the void will be found in the next book in this series, *Mike Mars at Cape Kennedy*. Look for it.